His voice dropped to a husky grumble, close to her face. "You play dirty."

"You'll never know…" Her mouth formed the whispered words with alluring deliberation.

That did it.

Those three simple words sent him over the edge, and the muscles in his legs started to twitch. He wobbled. His feet began to slip on the mat. Hell, even he had his limits. He managed to shift the bulk of his weight a split second before he landed on her, and their bodies became a tangle of limbs on the ground.

There was loud cheering and clapping in the background as Finn looked up into Shane's face with a look of pure glee. *"Loser."*

With her lush body entangled with his and his chest cushioned against her breasts he wasn't entirely sure that was true.

THE
FIREFIGHTER'S
CHOSEN BRIDE

TRISH WYLIE

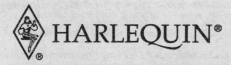

HARLEQUIN®

TORONTO • NEW YORK • LONDON
AMSTERDAM • PARIS • SYDNEY • HAMBURG
STOCKHOLM • ATHENS • TOKYO • MILAN • MADRID
PRAGUE • WARSAW • BUDAPEST • AUCKLAND

ISBN-13: 978-0-373-82056-6
ISBN-10:   0-373-82056-9

THE FIREFIGHTER'S CHOSEN BRIDE

First North American Publication 2007.

Previously published in the U.K. under the title *White Hot!*.

www.eHarlequin.com

Printed in U.S.A.

THE FIREFIGHTER'S CHOSEN BRIDE

For Finn. Who let me borrow her first name…

CHAPTER ONE

'I HAVE new carpet coming next week.'

Shane laughed. 'Not any more you don't.'

'It's cappuccino.'

'You bought coffee?'

'No, the carpet colour.' Finn nudged him hard in the ribs. 'It's cappuccino. That's what it's called.'

'I'm sure it'll be lovely on the lawn.'

There wasn't anywhere else left to put it.

'We might have stood a chance of catching it if you hadn't thrown vodka on it.'

Finn grimaced. 'I thought it was water.'

'Water would have been better. Though to be honest it would have taken more than a glass of the stuff.'

'All right, wise ass. But if you didn't have all that expensive training that I, as a tax-payer, *paid for* then you might have thrown the first thing that came to hand at it too.'

'I might have remembered what I was drinking before I went to bed.'

'*I* wasn't drinking it.'

Shane's dark eyebrows rose. 'Oh, really? Do tell.'

There were times when Shane Dwyer's way of asking a question accompanied with a mischievous sparkle in his blue eyes just bugged the hell out of Finn. Standing freezing to death in her pyjamas on a wintry December evening while her house was on fire was one of them. The fact that to answer him would involve a foray into her disastrous love life didn't help any.

She smirked at him.

After a brief burst of deep laughter, he inclined his head. 'C'mon, babe, move back a wee bit more.'

She stood statue-still on the pavement for another second as she looked at her house, eyes wide and blinking.

After all, a moment like this one deserved a little reflection, didn't it? She should be thinking deep and meaningful thoughts, contemplating twists of fate and the flammable quality of racks of underwear set to dry in front of a fireplace. Even *with* a fireguard.

Though, in hindsight, throwing the burnt-out candle ends on the open fire before she went to bed probably hadn't been a Mensa moment.

If only she'd forked out for a tumble dryer. But it had been a choice between a tumble dryer and nice carpet. And carpet had won…

'Finn?'

She found herself curious about the stupidest things. Had she put away her ironing? Had the DVD recorder taped the show she'd set it for before she'd left on her date? If she'd thought to have a selection of mixers available for her date would there even have been a glass of neat vodka for her to throw at the flames?

'*Finn.*' The deep voice became more demanding of her attention. 'C'mon, look at me a minute.'

Turning her head, she had to tilt her chin up to look into his familiar blue eyes. She could see many things there when she searched. She could see concern, warmth, sincerity. Obviously her taxes hadn't been wasted on his training in the customer service department.

She scowled at him. 'I'm having a moment here.'

He grinned down at her, white teeth glinting in his dirt-smeared face. Then he reached a gloved hand out to touch her arm. 'You go right on and take that moment. Don't let the chance of smoke inhalation ruin it for you.' He winked. 'Eddie is on his way; he'll be here any minute.'

He'd called Eddie already? That was nice of him, considerate even. Not to mention above and beyond the call of duty. But then it wasn't everybody whose house was burning down that had connections to the local fire brigade as Fionoula McNeill did.

Her brother Eddie was third generation after all.

Technically she'd now broken new ground by being the first generation to actually *start* a fire, so it would be sad if her brother missed it, right?

Shane continued to grin. 'It's almost all done here anyway. Then we'll get you home to our place, babe.'

Babe. He kept calling her *babe*, didn't he? Somewhere in her addled brain she allowed the endearment to slip through where it rattled around in her skull for a while and then seeped down into her chest. She'd have paid good money to hear him call her that in that tone before.

It was an awful shame it had taken her house to burn down for him to use it, *on her*. He never had trouble using the word on any other female on the island they called home. Finn *knew*.

It was a throwaway word for him, thrown mostly at skinny blondes with skirts so short they probably had permanent kidney infections, as it happened.

Knowing that meant it shouldn't have had any effect on Finn. But it did, it made her feel as if she had his full and undivided attention. Which didn't suck. Though the smoothing of his hand on her arm should have been more than enough to tell her she did even without the sexy sparks in his eyes.

If she'd just known all it would take was for her to burn her own house down…well, *damn*. Mentally she clicked her fingers at the missed opportunity.

Apparently sarcasm was her way of coping in a crisis. She sighed. Oh, well, it had always worked for everything else, why would this be any different?

Her eyes focused on his hand as she cleared her throat and managed an eloquent, 'Thanks.'

'No problem. I keep tellin' you I'm one hell of a guy, don't I?'

'That you do. But I'm wearing entirely too much for you to waste time flirting with me.'

'Oh, I dunno.' He lifted the hand from her arm and tilted his helmet back on his head. 'It's kinda sexy.'

Folding his arms across his wide chest, he let his eyes drop to stare openly at her breasts. Finn's chin dropped and then she looked upwards and rolled her eyes.

Shane lifted a hand and rubbed his chin. 'The hedgehog knows that's a brush, it's—'

'That's the whole joke, so, yes.' Well, if she'd known there would be a half-dozen guys to look at what she wore in bed most nights she'd maybe have planned better. Maybe. 'If it was another hedgehog it was doing it to it wouldn't be as funny, would it?'

'Still, you gotta wonder if it's not—' he paused for a second and then smiled his beautiful lazy smile '—a little *uncomfortable* for hedgehogs.'

Her eyes focused on his smile and then his lips and where they'd be if she took a step forward. *Tempting*. But it would be a bad case of any port in a storm. This was Shane Dwyer; they'd been dancing around each other for a while. So long as it never became a horizontal mambo she'd be just fine.

With a lift of her chin and a quirk of her head she smiled sweetly. 'They manage. And thanks so much for helping put out the fire and all. Another day at the office all wrapped up.'

Something flickered across his eyes when she looked back at him. 'Mmm.' His voice dropped an octave as he stepped closer, inclining his head towards her ear, 'Just don't go tryin' to burn down any more houses, babe. I don't like thinkin' someone that matters to me might be hurt.'

Huh? Her eyes widened.

Oh, well, this was just great. Her house, her first ever house as a home-owner, the one she'd made less than flipping seven mortgage repayments on, was burnt to a crisp in front of her by her own hands. And now she was reading between lines.

If her brother didn't get here soon she'd no doubt be imagining Shane professing undying love, throwing her over one of his broad shoulders and taking her back to his cave somewhere to distract her from her woes with hours of wanton—

'*Finn!*' Another voice sounded behind her. 'Finn, are you all right?'

Shane stepped back as Eddie grabbed her and pulled her into a bear hug that knocked her held breath from her lungs.

'I'll be fine so long as you don't crush me to death.'

'What the hell happened? Shane said someone made the call from a mobile?'

'I called it in.' She looked up into eyes the same green shade as her own. 'It happened very fast.'

'Where *were* you?' He stepped back and placed his large hands on her shoulders, shaking her gently. 'What the hell happened? Did you leave those damn straighteners plugged in again?'

'No! I didn't leave the damn straighteners plugged in again.' She shrugged free from his hold, her chin rising indignantly that he felt the need to give out to her when *her house had just been on fire*!

Then she glanced at Shane and saw his shoulders shuddering in barely suppressed laughter. Damn him! If she didn't tell her brother then he would, wouldn't he?

She looked back at Eddie's face and fluttered her eyelashes at him, pouting. It was worth a try. '*Anyone* could have made the same mistake.'

'You set fire to your own house?' Eddie glanced across at Shane as he hid his mouth behind a glove. But his eyes told the tale. 'Bloody hell, Finn.'

Her temper sparked. 'It's not like I planned on it! It was an accident. Why would I want to see my own house on fire? I ordered carpet, for crying out loud!'

'Yeah, espresso.'

'Cappuccino!' She glared at Shane.

'How many times have I told you about being careful?'

Finn scowled at her brother and opened her mouth to speak.

But as Shane stepped forward and placed a friendly arm around Eddie's shoulders he beat her to it. 'Hey, ease up. She did try to put it out.'

Son-of-a—

'You tried to put it *out*?' Eddie's face was incredulous. 'You stupid—'

He paused and took a breath. 'What did you do—throw a pan of water on it?'

'Not exactly.'

Shane lowered his voice and choked out the words, 'Think smaller.'

'Shut up, Shane.'

He laughed out loud, 'Oh, c'mon! You think the lads at the station aren't gonna pull his leg about this one for years? The least you can do is give him the heads up.'

'What did you do?'

With a scowl at Shane and a purse of her lips she jumped on in. 'It was the first thing that came to hand.'

'What was?'

'A glass of vodka.'

Eddie's mouth gaped at Shane's words. But before he could gather up a head of steam Finn added, 'It *looked* like water. Kevin must have left it on the side before we went out for dinner.'

'Who's Kevin?'

'My date.'

'What'd you do, send him out for a can of petrol?' Eddie pointed down the street.

'Don't be ridiculous!' She glared at them both one final time and started to march past them, her head held high.

They turned and fell into step on either side of her.

'How was the date, then?' Shane's deep voice sounded to her left.

She stopped, gaped at him for a second and then decided he was making with the funnies, so she stormed onwards. 'Ha, ha.'

She cleared her throat. 'Just tell the guys I appreciate what *they* did, will you, Shane?'

'No problem.' He glanced across at the rest of the crew as they began rolling up hoses and packing away equipment. 'I better go anyway.'

Eddie nodded across at him as they stopped by his Jeep. 'I'll take her on back to the house.'

'Probably best; she's too calm about this.'

'Probably shock.'

Shane nodded. 'Probably.'

'Could you two stop talking about me like I'm not here?' She glared at them in turn. 'I hate it when you do that.'

'We know.'

She glared harder when they answered in unison. 'Well, knock it on the head, then.'

'We're just concerned about you, is all.' Eddie smiled. 'Would you prefer it if we yanked out some marshmallows on sticks?'

'Yeah, we keep bags of them on the truck, you know that.' Shane's face was deadpan but his eyes sparkled.

'You're both hilarious.'

'Babe, we're only trying to take your mind off it.' He reached out a large gloved hand again and squeezed her upper arm, his eyes focused on hers. 'This is a big thing that's happened here and you're gonna need a little time to deal with it. All joking aside, you've lost a lot.'

They could be too protective when they wanted to be. She knew how big a deal what had happened was. She gave a little laugh, but a chill suddenly radiated through every inch of her body at the thought of what could have been. 'There's not much to deal with that I can see. I have no home, no clothes, in fact everything I own bar what I have on and what's in the car is now a great smoking pile of ash. Seems pretty straightforward to me.'

It was the wobble on the last few words that brought her sarcasm to a halt and she knew Shane had caught them too when a small scowl appeared on his forehead.

He released her arm and stepped back, his voice firm as he glanced at Eddie. 'Take her home. I'll be back before you go on shift in the morning and I'll look out for her.'

Oh, yeah, that would help no end. Stuck inside four walls with Shane 'looking out for her'. Her throat threatened to close over and she could feel tears prickling at the back of her eyes as hysteria rose in her chest.

This was a disaster. It really was.

When she spoke her voice was brittle. 'I don't need looking after and I have *work* in the morning.'

'The hell you do.'

'You're not going to work.'

She scowled when they spoke in unison again. 'Yes, I am! I need to earn a wage to pay for wee things like clothes, seeing as I don't have any any more.'

'We'll lend you some.'

While Shane nodded in agreement with Eddie's statement Finn quietly fumed. It felt better to be angry with them than to focus on what had just happened and the repercussions of it on her calm and organized world. Typical macho men—it just wouldn't occur to them that she might see anything hurtful in the fact that they believed their clothes would *fit* her!

Add that to talking over her, joking about marshmallows and the fact that she now had to go stay in Shane's house…

Well, hell, why didn't they just give her a nice paper cut and some lemon juice?

'C'mon, Finn, let's get you back home and I'll make you some sweet tea. You'll feel better then.'

Sure she would. Tea was the cure for all ills, after all. As her brother cupped her elbow and guided her away from the burnt ruin of her house she glanced back over her shoulder. She couldn't help herself.

But her eyes didn't stray to the house for long. Without thought, they sought out Shane where he stood watching them walk away. And the bubble of hysteria returned.

She didn't want to be stuck under the same roof as him. She really didn't. Why was someone somewhere punishing her for the loss of her house? She really hadn't burned it down on purpose, even if she had truly hated the carpet and bright yellow doors gave her migraine.

Staying with Shane had the possibility of being an even worse disaster than her house burning down.

CHAPTER TWO

A YELLING voice woke Shane up.

When he'd got back home after his shift he'd only had a few moments to get an update from Eddie on how Finn was.

'Still too calm if you ask me,' Eddie stated. 'I gave her a good dose of whiskey in some tea before she went to bed and she's been fairly sound since she drifted off. But I don't think it's hit yet.'

Shane smiled, 'So long as she didn't try to throw it on any flames, eh?'

Eddie laughed. 'It could only happen to Finn, you know. When disaster strikes her it's as subtle as an elephant in a tutu.' His smile faded. 'She has to be cut up, though.'

Shane stared his best friend straight in the eye. 'She's not made of stone and she worked her ass off for that house.'

'Yeah, well, I rang her work and they know she'll not be in for a while. Keep an eye out.'

So he'd settled himself on the sofa, reckoning that way he would hear when she woke up and started moving around. If he knew Finn she'd try to sneak out to work.

The next thing he was aware of was the sound of her voice calling out, pulling him from the depths of slumber.

It got louder as he ran upstairs two steps at a time.

'No!'

He was at her door in a few more steps.

'It's too hot. Get out! Out of the fire!'

'Finn.' He sat down beside her, his weight dipping the mattress and rolling her body towards him. 'Finn, wake up.'

When he reached a hand to her arm she stirred and her eyes shot open, widening at the sight of him, 'Shane! What the hell—?'

'You were yelling.'

'No, I wasn't.' She struggled into a sitting position, instinctively drawing the duvet up with her like a protective shield. 'I was asleep.'

'Then you were dreaming.' His hand smoothed along her arm until it met her hand and squeezed gently. 'You were calling to get out of the fire.'

The touch of his hand had momentarily drawn her attention but his words drained the colour from her face. 'No, I wasn't.'

'Yeah, you were.'

The soft tone in his deep voice made her heart twist nearly as painfully as her dream had. There was no use denying it; if Shane said she'd called out about a fire, then she had. Thing was, she hadn't had the dream in years. Not since she'd been a kid.

She took a moment to compose herself, determined not to go all weepy and girly when he smiled a gentle smile at her. It was just a natural reaction to her house burning down, was all. She was overly sensitive. Understandably. But damned if she would show it in front of *him*.

His hand tightened on hers. 'You okay?'

'I'm fine.' She tugged her hand free before the warmth his touch created could work its way up her arm, then shuffled ungracefully off the other side of the bed. 'What time is it? I can't be late for work.'

'Eddie already rang in for you.' His eyes followed her movement around the room, drawn of their own accord to the long length of naked leg beneath the oversized T-shirt she wore. Well, it couldn't be helped really, he was a legs man, after all. Old habits and all that.

When she swung to face him she caught him looking and a flush crept up her neck. Her hands lowered in a reflex action to the hem of the T-shirt where she tugged. As if the action would somehow make it floor-length. Suddenly she wished she'd kept on the pyjamas that had stunk of smoke. 'What do you mean he rang in for me? I'm not twelve years old. And I can't miss a day at work. We're busy, for crying out loud. It's December; we do a third of a—'

'Year's business in one month.' He nodded, continuing to look at her legs from shapely ankles upwards. 'You tell us that every year. We nearly know the music distribution business as well as you do now.'

'Well, it's true. This is just about the worst time of year for me to be off.' Her eyes dragged away from his face as she searched frantically for something to cover her legs with. Then she stopped looking and scowled. This was supposedly *her* room while she stayed in his house. Who was *he* to come in uninvited, to hear things he had no right hearing, that would no doubt need an explanation she wasn't ready to give, and to then openly ogle her? And even more to the point how dared he raise her pulse rate doing it?

'Could you kindly leave now?'

His eyes rose slowly to meet hers. 'I only came up 'cos you sounded upset. I was being a gentleman.'

Finn snorted gracefully. 'Well, I'm not upset, I'm fine. And you're not being a gentleman; you're staring at my legs is what you're doing.'

He smiled. 'What can I say? There's a lot of leg to look at.'

And with that his eyes flickered back down. Finn felt her flush working its way up off her neck onto her cheeks, felt her pulse beating harder in the base of her throat. It was ridiculous. It wasn't as if Shane Dwyer hadn't ever looked at her before. It was just she hadn't been semi-naked, *sans* underwear at the time. Or alone in a bedroom with him. Which hadn't happened *ever.*

'So is this what you do to look out for someone when they've been through a traumatic experience? Ogle them?'

The smile was slow and sensual, accompanied by a twinkle in the blue of his eyes as he looked back at her face. 'Only when they have legs like yours, babe.'

Finn stared in blatant disbelief.

'Taken your mind off your bad dream, though, hasn't it?'

Brute. But he was right. The dream had sneaked into her mind in that period of sleep between deep, dreamless slumber and wakening and she knew the memory of it would stay with her even now that she was completely awake. If she wasn't being distracted by other things.

Even mentioning it brought it back. And it still ached. An ache on top of an ache of old unless she was very much mistaken. Which was all she needed! His quiet study of her had taken that ache from her chest and moved it in a more southerly direction, that much was true. But it didn't stop her from being ticked at him.

Because now that he'd pointed out how it had been a purposeful distraction ploy, the ache moved into her mind like a dull headache, where the recent memory was still as clear as a picture on a cinema screen.

'Right then, seeing as you're wide awake now and *fine*—' Shane stood up and walked towards the doorway, his naked feet silent on the carpeted floor '—throw something on and we'll go take a look at your house.'

Finn's eyes widened. 'What would we do that for? There's not much point seeing as it's gone.'

'You still need to see it, though.'

'I don't think I do.'

'Well, *I* do—' he turned at the doorway and looked her right in the eyes, his own silently determined '—and I've been doing this kind of thing longer than you have. So get dressed and I'll take you shopping afterwards for being a good girl. Get you some clothes.'

The shopping was certainly a necessity. But she didn't need him to take her, she could take herself. The independent woman in her rebelled at his bossy, patronizing attitude. Up until a few hours ago she'd had no one to answer to. No one who felt she needed babysitting in case she dissolved into a crumpled heap of despair.

But then a few hours ago she'd had pyjama bottoms, and plenty of underwear that wasn't used to burn her own house down...

As his eyes swept again to her legs and a dimple appeared in his cheek to accompany a roguish lopsided smile she decided she'd let herself be led, just this once. Out of necessity.

Then she would find somewhere else to live. Where she couldn't be ogled by six feet two of dangerously distracting male.

* * *

It was a mess. With Shane at her side she picked her way tentatively through the sodden heaps that made up all of her earthly possessions.

Then it started to hit her, the stark reality of what had happened. She was picking her way through her life. Her own carelessness had destroyed everything. She could have died drying practical cotton underwear on a rack by the fire. Not even nice underwear, though G-strings might not have caught fire so easily, but honest to goodness large flammable pants could have killed her.

Put that one on a gravestone…

Leaning down, she pulled a blackened picture frame from the floor, her trembling fingers brushing dirt back from the glass to reveal the faces of her family. The first stroke revealed her brother Niall's face, then Conor, then Eddie, then a small pony-tailed version of herself. Then she could see her mother's smile before her fingers finally revealed her father's beaming face.

Her throat closed over and she had to blink hard to hold hot tears at bay. Damn it. Damned stupid fires.

Shane had been looking around at the structure itself, while he stood a few feet away from her. The house was old, and the interior had taken a beating in the fire. But the structure still looked pretty sound to him, the walls all still in place. He would never have asked permission to bring them in otherwise. But it would cost a fortune to rebuild. Finn would probably be better cutting her losses on it. 'You have house insurance, right?'

She cleared her throat. 'Yes, and contents.'

He continued to survey the room. 'Good. You'll be all right, then. It wasn't like you did this on purpose. We'll go get the paperwork started this afternoon and then that'll be one less thing for you to worry about.'

When his eyes found Finn again she had her back turned to him, her head slumped forward. He stepped closer, his voice softening. 'You okay?'

She lifted a hand and swiped at the tears that had escaped from her eyes before he could see them. 'I'm fine.'

Another photograph caught her eye, the glass shattered inside the frame. Hunching down, she shook the glass out and looked at the singed picture. It was one that had sat on a wide window sill, had had pride of place, of Eddie and Shane on the day they had become fully fledged firefighters.

Between their equally large frames was Finn, a huge grin on her face as they all hammed it up for the camera.

The air displaced behind her as Shane got close and she shivered involuntarily as he spoke over her shoulder. 'That was a grand day. We all went out on the tear after, remember?'

Finn nodded, her voice low. 'Then after a few drinks you both spent the evening demonstrating your fireman's lifts with single women in the bar.'

'Before Eddie got that twinge in his back.'

'And you told him his career was over before it had even started.'

'I was wrong there; he's saved dozens of cats since then.' His eyes studied the back of her head as she stood up, then he reached a hand to her shoulder and turned her to face him. His gaze narrowed briefly. 'This is tough, babe, I know, but there might be a few other things you can save. Take your time.'

She couldn't look up at him, her focus remaining on the picture. 'I'm f—'

'I swear, Finn, if you say "fine" one more time I'm

gonna have to kick you.' One long finger tilted her chin up and he studied her face with a small smile. 'It's okay to not be fine when it's something this big.'

'No, it's not.' The smile she gave him was unconvincing. 'I'm a firefighter's daughter, a firefighter's sister, and I just set fire to my own house.'

He kept smiling. 'It's not like you're planning on taking up a career as an arsonist, though, is it? It was an accident, that's all. Give yourself a break.'

'I know that. I do. No one got hurt and I hadn't bought a cat yet so it's not that big a deal really.'

'This house was a big deal when you got word you'd bought it. It was a big deal when we all helped you move in. It was such a big deal when you had your first dinner party that we even used napkins.' He reached his free hand to the smears she probably didn't even know she'd made on her cheek and rubbed at them with a roughened thumb. 'You worked hard for this place and everyone was proud of what you'd achieved. You should go right on ahead and be sorry it happened; you just shouldn't blame yourself. That's all.'

It was quite a speech for Shane, and they both knew it.

'You've owned a house for years—' she managed a smile '—and you've not set fire to it. So you're way ahead of me.'

Yeah, but he hadn't had to work to buy his house. It had been a final gift from his mother. Finn had worked for hers, he had watched her do it and could never remember being so proud of anyone before.

He studied her face for a long moment, then tugged her roughly into his arms and held her against his broad chest as she gave in to silent tears. 'I'm fully versed in the dangers of underwear.' He chuckled. 'It could have happened to anyone who wasn't trained. You were unlucky, is all. Just unlucky.'

She allowed the warmth of his body to seep through to her chilled bones. Felt a sense of safety being held by him that she couldn't remember having felt in a long time and she let her fears slip out in response. 'If someone had got hurt I don't know what I'd have—'

He interrupted her again, accompanying the words with a tightening of his arms. 'Quit it now; no one got hurt. So there's not much point torturing yourself over it. You're okay and that's what matters.'

'Thank you.' She didn't know what else to say to him. He was right, so matter-of-fact and practical about it, but still understanding how much owning the house had meant to her, yellow doors and flowery carpet and all; buying it had been her first major achievement. She *had* worked hard for it, damn hard. And even though she knew the insurance would take care of everything it still didn't make up for all the things she'd lost. Things that might have seemed trivial to someone else but had held memories for her. Like pictures of her dad that couldn't be replaced.

That was probably what her dream had been about.

But even though she appreciated what Shane was trying to do for her, and how being held in his arms made her feel cared for, she had to pull herself together and step away from him. She couldn't go getting all gooey around him or allowing herself to get used to being held. That would be bad.

Because she had found it difficult enough to mentally keep him at arm's length for the last while, had discovered a new-found fascination for him that wasn't exactly platonic. Which was *b-a-d*.

He allowed her to get as far as half an arm's length. 'You want to look around for some more pictures and stuff?'

'Yeah, that would be good.'

'We'll salvage what we can and then we'll go get you some new clothes.'

'When these are so attractive?' She used it as an excuse to pull free, looking down at the oversize sweater and jogging pants that Eddie had left out for her. She laughed wryly, trying to ease the tension she felt. 'I feel like someone on the end of a massive weight loss diet.'

'Well they're not as sexy as the hedgehog was, right enough.' He grinned when she pulled a face. 'But I bet we can do better. Think of it as an opportunity to revamp your wardrobe.'

Finn arched an eyebrow. 'There was something wrong with my wardrobe before?'

'No-o, not exactly.' He turned and began to look around at the crowded floor again, leaning down to push aside some sodden cushions. 'But you could be a bit too strait-laced, y'know. You should loosen up some.'

Strait-laced? He thought she was *strait-laced?* That kind of a statement would have been enough to make her want to prove him wrong, if he'd been anyone else. 'So I should take this opportunity to buy things a little more *slutty?*'

He glanced up at her from beneath long dark lashes, his eyes glinting dangerously. 'Well, hell, Finn, now I *really* want to go shopping.'

'Oh, I'll bet. You'll have me in miniskirts and fishnet stockings before I can blink an eye.'

'You run around my place wearing miniskirts and fishnets and I might not be held accountable for my actions. I'm only human.'

Finn gaped. He was flirting with her? Shane Dwyer superhero, was *only human*?

Not that he hadn't turned on the charm around her before. But he'd never been so brazen about it. She shook her head. *Nah*. He was just trying to distract her again, that was all.

Proving very good at it, as it happened.

'Very funny, Dwyer.' She pointed across the room. 'You can just go over there and look for more photos and I'll stay over here where I won't bump into your ego.'

The laughter was deep and melodious, filling the silent wreck of her house as he moved away.

After a moment she smiled too. She couldn't help herself. It was nice of him to try distracting her, even if his method was so outrageous. And for a split second she even wondered what would happen if she flirted back.

Ah, well. Every girl had to have an imagination. It was healthy, right?

Half an hour later they both had armfuls of photos, a few ornaments that had survived, and Finn turned to him, feeling a little easier. 'You don't have to come shopping. We can go back to the house and I'll get my car. You're bound to be tired after being on night shift.'

She looked across at the dark shadow of stubble on his cheeks and the lazy blink of his eyes. He *was* tired; she could see it. His being so easy to look at meant she could read his face pretty well after years of intensive study.

Green eyes continued their study as he moved across to her side again, picking his way over piles of wet furniture and burnt curtains with confident steps. She'd always been aware of how he looked; it wouldn't have taken her house to have burned down for her to have noticed. But she'd never really spent any time alone in his company to allow herself the luxury of studying him closely enough to see beneath the surface.

He took up a large space on the planet, which would have drawn any woman's gaze in his direction. At a rock concert he would never have any difficulties seeing the band on stage. Mind you, neither would Finn. It was probably the first reason she'd had for looking at him. At five eight, she wasn't exactly a leprechaun herself. Which meant taller guys caught her attention.

Then add to the height a devastating combination of black hair and startling blue eyes, dimples and disgustingly white, straight teeth and, *well*…

She wondered for the gazillionth time just how in God's name someone who looked like him managed to stay single. Women certainly had never had any problems falling at his feet. Finn could even guess at how many. Not that she'd kept a score card or anything.

Watching his approach she wondered if he could actually be that guy who kept notches on his bedpost. While she was in his house she could take a look. For curiosity's sake, not because she wanted to see the inside of his bedroom. Well, okay, she wouldn't mind seeing if he had black silk sheets and a leopard-skin printed throw on a water-bed. That would be evidence enough.

He stopped right in front of her and winked. 'I wouldn't miss this shopping trip for the world.'

'Oh, I'll bet.' She leaned her head a little closer. 'Though if you insist on going, you should know: *I'll* be picking the clothes. You can carry bags. That's what guys are for on shopping trips.'

Shane grinned when she smirked at him. 'I think you'll find we're for way more than that.' He laughed as she narrowed her eyes. 'Think of it as an opportunity to get a male perspective on what you wear.'

'Yeah, right.'

'Where's your sense of adventure? You've been hiding under business suits and rugby shirts for as long as I've known you.'

Hiding was right. She wasn't exactly a perfect size ten, after all, and she certainly didn't want to encourage him to look at anything other than her bare legs. But the last thing she needed was Shane helping her pick out a new wardrobe. Not if he was going to spend the whole afternoon flirting with her as he did it. 'I wear clothes that are appropriate for the things I do and, seeing as how most of the time I'm either working or hanging around with you losers, then what I normally wear is just fine.'

Shane leaned in so that his nose almost touched hers, his warm breath fanning out across her face. '*Chicken.*'

She had to resist the urge to step away from him. But she was damned if she'd let him see she was affected by how close his face was to hers. How all it would take would be a small tilt and a tiny lean forward and she could kiss the sensual curve of his mouth to shut him up. *If she'd been someone else*

But she would *not* be intimidated and she would *not* be called a chicken. He had advantage enough by the very fact that she kept looking at him and thinking the way she was. 'One outfit.'

His eyes blinked slowly as he continued to smile. 'One?'

'You can help pick out one outfit that won't get me arrested and that's it. Then you'll never criticize my wardrobe again. Deal?'

The challenge in her voice and the raise of her chin

brought his dimples out in force. He leaned back and reached a hand forward, waiting for her to add hers for a shake to seal the deal. With her hand enclosed in his he dropped his voice an intimate octave. 'Deal.' But when she smiled smugly and tried to tug her hand away he held on for another second to add, 'And underwear.' He laughed as she gaped in outrage. 'It's not like you have any left, after all. And if you're gonna live in my house you should have some, don't you think?'

When she continued to gape he shrugged. 'Consider it an early Christmas present. Otherwise you'll end up wandering around with me looking at more than just your legs.'

CHAPTER THREE

WELL, if it was Shane's way of continuing to distract her, it was certainly working. House fire? *What* house fire, *where*?

Though Finn wasn't overly keen on her reaction to the female sales assistants that radiated to him in the middle of the exclusive underwear store he found in Dublin city centre. In fact, any shop they visited that had female assistants under the age of eighty seemed to end up with the same result. As if it weren't *Finn* that was shopping.

Talk about bees round honey! The minute the bell over the door jingled they all looked his way. And Finn might as well have been invisible.

She scowled across at him. It was the most ridiculous shopping trip she'd ever been on in her entire life. Trust a man to ruin *shopping*!

'Can I help you?'

Oh, Finn would just bet she'd love to *help* him! No doubt hanging naked from a chandelier if he asked her to.

Stepping between them she smiled a sugary-sweet smile. 'We're just browsing.'

'No, we're not.' Shane placed an arm around her waist and squeezed in warning. 'We're shopping.'

'No, *we're* not.' She smiled through gritted teeth. '*I* am. He's just here to carry bags.'

'Not in here I'm not, babe.'

The 'babe' thing was really starting to grate on her nerves. Especially when he accompanied the word meant for her with a winning smile aimed at the assistants. She had managed to grit her teeth through three stores so far but the underwear thing was where she was determined to draw the line. No matter what he thought.

Extricating herself from his hold, she aimed a sickly sweet smile in his direction. 'Yes, you are. You can stand here and talk to these nice ladies while I pick up the basic essentials and then we're outta here.'

'She gets all embarrassed when I pick underwear for her.'

'Surely not,' one svelte blonde purred across at him. 'Women love it when good-looking men like yourself pick out something special for them.'

Something that would no doubt be stupidly uncomfortable and designed to be worn in a bedroom for thirty seconds, and not all day underneath one of the new business suits she'd just bought.

How exactly had she been conned into this again?

'You'd have thought so, wouldn't you?' Shane continued to smile at the assistants. 'But Finn is a little shy when it comes to this kind of thing.'

Because Finn had never actually thought about wearing '*this* kind of thing'. Her eyes widened as he pointed at a dummy displaying a teeny garment that seemed to be made of lace and dental floss.

'This one is nice.' He stepped closer and ran his finger under a strap, his eyes moving over the head of the assistant to clash with Finn's. 'Don't you think, babe?'

The tone was seduction itself and Finn felt her body respond with an immediate surge of heat while her eyes focused on the finger playing with the strap. For a brief moment her imagination painted a picture of the finger caught between the strap and her skin. Then the finger would gently slip the strap from her shoulder, the material would whisper down over her breasts.

He smiled a knowing smile as she blew out a puff of air. So she answered with a scowl.

He was a dead man. That was what she thought.

'I prefer this.' She nonchalantly dangled something more practical above her head.

'Now, remember we talked about your sense of adventure?'

'Yes, and remember we also promised that we would buy you something to wear the same as I get only in red?'

She leaned closer to the only assistant still beside her and hissed, 'I swear he has more heels at home than I do.'

The blonde assistant took a visible step back from him while Shane's eyes narrowed. 'We'll take this one.'

'In what size?' the blonde asked with a cool voice and Finn had to swallow a bubble of laughter.

The laughter then froze when he rhymed off her size after a flicker of his eyes down over her body. How could he *do* that?

He then raised a single eyebrow in challenge and began to walk amongst the displays, lifting items and running his fingers over their textures. 'And this, and one of these and two pairs of these and—'

'Whoa one minute, buster. We agreed one outfit.'

'C'mon, it's nearly Christmas and, anyway, you can't walk around half naked all the time.'

She had not been half naked! Not entirely. Pretty much naked, yes, but Eddie's T-shirt had covered everything that mattered, hadn't it? Except the legs Shane had been so interested in. The fact that he might have known she was all but naked kicked her imagination into gear again. Just what had he thought of that idea? What would he have done if he'd known for sure and taken it as an invitation? Just exactly how many moves had he picked up over the years? How long could he have kept them occupied?

She had a few moves of her own, after all…

All right-y, this *had* to stop. And she really had to get back to the house so she could ring all her friends and beg for a place to stay. A sofa would do.

Lifting a handful of less X-rated bras and knickers, she added them to the pile he'd been making and then pushed him back from the counter. '*Enough* already.'

His arm snaked around her waist and held her tightly in place at his side as he swung his credit card at the blonde with a cavalier sweep. 'On me.'

'No, I've got it.' She fumbled in her bag, which rubbed her rear a tad too deliciously against his hard frame. 'You're not buying all this underwear for me, Shane.'

'Yes, I am. It's worth every penny to see you so *hot* and bothered.'

The words were whispered close to her ear and the already rising warmth in her body hit boiling point. But when she tried to pull away from him he merely held on tighter. Strong as she was, she couldn't get away without making a massive scene. So she smiled through gritted teeth and turned to whisper back, 'I *owe* you.'

Shane's eyes danced. 'Just model some of this lot some time and we'll be even.'

'That's not what I meant I owed you for.'

The minute they left the store she swung the bag at him, hitting the centre of his chest.

He laughed and made a mock grunt of pain. 'Careful, now; you'll bruise me with all that heavy underwear.'

'You deserve a good bruising for that performance in there. You can just quit it now; you've done your job,' She raised her chin and walked with a determined stride along the wide pavement. 'I've been well and truly distracted from my arson problems all afternoon. So you can knock it on the head now.'

Shane had no problem keeping up with her fast pace, but the minute she finished speaking he caught her arm and tugged her round to face him. 'You think that's what I'm doing? *Distracting* you?'

The sudden change in direction had swung her hair into her face and the auburn ends caught in her mouth. With her free hand she plucked the ends free, frowning into his smiling face. 'You didn't think I'd figure it out? I may be many things, Shane Dwyer, but dumb isn't one of them.'

'I wouldn't have said so until now.' He cocked his head to one side, his bright blue eyes focused on her mouth as she cleared the last strands of hair. 'I'm not trying to distract you, Finn. If all this is taking your mind off other things, then that's great. But I hadn't thought about it that deeply. Sure as hell not since we started looking at underwear, anyway.'

Finn frowned in confusion. He wasn't trying to distract her? Then why was he flirting with her? Her eyes widened. He wouldn't dare…

The dimples flashed at her before he released her arm and sauntered ahead of her down the street. Whistling.

Whistling, for crying out loud!

* * *

After a full afternoon in Shane's company, one-entirely-
too-closely-on-one, she was more than grateful to get a call
from her best friend, Mel. After a half-hour's conversation
on her mobile about the fire, Mel decided that sweet tea
sucked and what she needed was to drown her sorrows in
a more traditional Irish manner.

And at least at O'Malley's she was out of the house and
away from Shane.

'So, what does Mr Sex-on-a-stick look like first thing
in the morning?'

Too damn good, as it happened. 'Can we talk about
something else?'

'Wow, that good, huh?' Mel waggled her eyebrows as
she raised her glass. 'Figures.'

'I keep telling you, if you think he's so hot then you
should just go for it.'

Her friend knew her too well. 'Yes, and I can tell from
that tone that you'd be chuffed to bits by that.'

Finn sighed. 'He can date whoever he wants, it's nothing
to do with me.'

'Mmm.'

'Don't do that.'

'What?' She blinked innocently.

Finn smiled at her amateur dramatics, 'You know what.
I've told you before, I'm not interested.'

'Uh-huh.' Mel's fingers swirled the plastic stirrer around
in her glass, tinkling ice cubes against the edges. 'But
that'd be a teeny bit of a fib, wouldn't it? Sometimes you
look at him like a choc-a-holic looks at a plate full of Death
By Chocolate.'

'Looking is one thing.'

Mel nodded wisely. 'So you have no problem when chesty women throw themselves at him?'

Finn laughed. 'Oh, honey, you're not chesty. We've talked about this loads and we've always said there was no danger of you getting black eyes if you took up jogging.'

'I wasn't talking about *me...*'

With a sinking feeling in the pit of her stomach, Finn turned on her tall stool and looked at the bar. Sure enough, Shane and Eddie were there and Shane had already attracted a chesty woman. His dimples still present from something she had said to him, his eyes rose and met hers.

Her breath caught as his eyes twinkled across at her. He really bloody did have the charm of the devil, didn't he?

With a scowl she turned back round to face her grinning friend. 'Don't say a word. Not one, y'hear?'

Mel held both hands up in front of her body. 'Silent as the grave over here.'

Finn downed a large mouthful of the concoction Mel had got her from the bar, her eyes watering slightly as she swallowed.

When she looked back at Mel she saw her eyes move upwards. Immediately she sat taller on her chair, her spine stiff as she waited for the air behind her to tingle as it had all afternoon.

A beer bottle appeared on the table in front of her. 'Drowning your sorrows?'

Exhaling the breath she was holding, she looked up at her brother. 'Don't you think I'd have good reason to?'

'Well, of all the lame excuses you two have used on a night out before I guess this would be one of the better ones.' He winked across at Mel. 'Hey, gorgeous.'

'Hey, Eddie. Kathy let you out on your own? She must reckon she has you well pinned down.'

'I'm not on my own; I'm with Shane.'

'And if ever there was a mate who could find you a woman to get you in trouble, it would be *him*.'

Eddie laughed. 'He's always been a babe magnet. Beats me how he does it.'

Finn could write him a list if he asked. She sat silently fuming for no apparent reason. 'Well, there better not be a string of them at the house while *I'm* there.'

'String of what?' Shane plunked himself onto the stool next to her. 'Hi, Mel.'

Mel practically batted her eyelashes at him. 'Hi, Shane.'

Eddie laughed as he lifted his beer bottle and Shane turned his body towards Finn, leaning his elbows on the table, which rocked it and had both women rescuing their glasses. 'String of what at the house while you're there?'

Finn searched her mind frantically for a suitable reply. But her brother beat her to it. 'She's afraid you're gonna bring a string of babes back to the house while she's there. Doesn't want you showing her how sad her own love life is.'

Shane's eyes had strayed to Eddie as he spoke but then his gaze slid slowly to her face. Lifting his elbows, he reclaimed his bottle and examined her above the rim for a long moment. 'Is your love life sad, Finn?'

'None of your business.' She smiled sweetly as she sipped her drink again. Forcing herself not to pull a face as the liquid seared her throat.

'Didn't you have a date before you had a late Halloween bonfire?'

Glaring at her brother, she sniped back, 'Thanks *so* much for bringing that up.'

'Oh, yeah, what's-his-name, the librarian. How'd that go?' Mel rattled her ice cubes again as her eyes sparkled.

'He's not a librarian; he's a clerical officer.'

'Same thing, isn't it?' Shane queried with a wink at Eddie.

Finn smirked. 'Not everyone suits the cape-and-tights look.'

Eddie laughed. 'At least if we got a ladder in our tights it could be put to some use.'

After simultaneous groans Mel quipped, 'Stuns me why you bother with all those librarians when you have a dating agency for a brother.'

'Finn doesn't date firefighters.'

'Too hot for you, Finn?'

Finn avoided looking into Shane's blue eyes again as he asked the question in a voice steeped in innuendo. She was suddenly more aware of the nuances in his voice than she had been before. She could chalk that one down to his flirting with her all afternoon, she guessed.

All right, so his use of the word 'hot' twice in one day had helped. He had a way of saying that word that went straight to the part of her body that then squirmed on her stool.

Lifting her glass to hide behind its rim, she glanced at Mel and her brother to see if they'd caught it too. Flirting with her when they were alone was one thing. A bad enough thing. But flirting openly in front of friends and family and getting her *squirmy* in public was worse.

'They'd have to get past me first,' Eddie said in a grim voice. 'I have to look out for my baby sister.'

Finn snorted into her glass. 'I feel *much* safer now.'

'You could always have your librarian fend them off with a good hard-backed book.'

The various defensive weapons available to a librarian

were discussed for a while as the bar began to fill up. Someone somewhere put dance music on the jukebox so their voices all rose accordingly and they had to lean their heads closer to hear. And all the while Finn was totally aware of where Shane was, of how his throat would convulse as he swallowed a mouthful of beer, of how his long fingers curled around the bottle.

At one point she even chanced a look at him while his head was turned towards Mel. She looked at the way he sat so easily on the tall stool, one foot resting on the floor, legs wide, his broad frame tall and lean. Any bit of wonder women in bars gravitated toward him!

Her eyes were on the broad column of his neck at the V of his polo shirt when she realized he had turned his face back towards her. She glanced upwards into eyes that looked black in the dim light of the bar. And he looked back at her with several lazy blinks of thick dark lashes.

Her throat went dry. With a small wave of panic her eyes flew to Mel, who smiled at her with a knowing look.

'Anyone want another drink?' Eddie's voice rose at her side. 'Mel, you'll take one. Shane, need I ask?'

'I'm grand.' Finn couldn't face another drink. She needed her wits about her.

'I'll come with you, Eddie.'

Finn glared at her soon to be 'ex' friend as she smiled on her way past.

'*So...*'

She took a deep breath as Shane's deep voice rumbled close to her ear. Leaning back a little on her chair, she turned her face towards him, blinking calmly. 'So?'

'Maybe we should have a chat about bringing people back to the house while you're staying there.'

'I'll not be staying all that long.'

'Still, if you're *bothered* about it, maybe we should discuss it. Set the boundaries.'

Jealousy swept through her chest like a hot knife through butter. It was one thing witnessing him surrounded by women on a night out, but she'd never had to think of him sleeping with someone under the same roof as her. It was none of her business. And it was *his* house. She had no right to dictate to a grown man what he could and couldn't do, did she? And it really shouldn't matter. But—

Lying in the dark listening to them? Oh, 'cos there'd *be* noise, she'd bet—

'Do what you want. It's nothing to do with me.'

She knew his eyes were still on her as she turned her face away and squirmed again.

'I have no intention of bringing anyone home.'

Oh, no. Now, y'see, *that* was worse. With a groan she looked back at him, determined to tell him it really didn't matter a damn to her only to have him add, 'And if you even think of it I'll probably break his neck and chuck him out on the street.'

Her mouth dropped open.

Shane shrugged, a small smile twitching the corners of his mouth as he lifted his bottle again. 'Just so you know.'

Not that she would have. Not that she actually had any candidates or had done in a long, long while. The very fact that he thought he could just say something like that and get away with it…

'Like I said, I won't be there all that long.'

He seemed to think for a while as he swallowed and set his bottle back down, folding his arms across his chest in a way that highlighted the muscles in his upper arms. 'Don't know that it would make a difference even if you moved out. Not now that we've bought underwear together.'

'Why, you—' She found herself lost for words, again. Then did the only thing she could think of and reached an arm out to shove him.

The stool wobbled; he had to set his other foot on the floor to balance himself. And as he did he swiftly unfolded his arms and caught her hand in his.

She laughed at the momentary panic that had crossed his face. 'You deserved that.'

Turning her hand in his, he tangled his long fingers with hers and held on, leaning closer with dangerously glittering eyes. 'You know one of the first things a boy learns in the playground is that when a girl hits him it means she likes him?'

Finn shook her head, a smile still on her lips while he guided their joined hands below the table. 'Jeez, and you actually get laid with these chat-up lines?'

It was Shane's turn to laugh. 'It's worked before.'

'You really need to date women with an IQ above fifty, you know.'

His eyes flickered to one side, then back to hers. Then he nodded. 'Oh, don't worry, babe, I'm thinking about it. I've been thinking about it *plenty*.'

He released her hand a second before Eddie placed drinks on the table. 'What did I miss?'

CHAPTER FOUR

THE damn dream came again just before dawn.

Clearer and more real than it had been the night before. This time Finn could feel the thick smoke burning the back of her throat and making her eyes sting.

She felt the heat against her face, heard the crashing close by as bits of ceiling fell down. But it was too dark for her to see the figure clearly.

She pushed a door open and flames jumped out at her and then she could see the shadow of him as he pushed through the room, an oxygen mask covering his face.

'Get out of there. You have to get out.' She could barely call the words out, her throat burned so badly.

'It's too hot!' She held her arm above her face as another flame rushed at her. Opening her eyes again, she could just see the roof cave above his head. 'No!'

And then she was awake. Sat bolt upright in her bed with her new nightdress soaked in perspiration and clinging to her body.

She sat in the dark room, holding her breath in case Shane appeared beside her again. Then she exhaled. This was getting ridiculous. Maybe if she'd had clearer thoughts when she'd gone to bed in the first place. Maybe if she'd not been so worried about when she could find herself somewhere new to live. Maybe…

Ah, heck, who was she kidding? Maybe if she hadn't already been *hotter than hell* going to bed she wouldn't have had the dream about heat of a different kind.

Whatever the fixation she had with Shane was, it had to go. There was no way she could allow herself to get involved with him. There were a million different reasons why she shouldn't.

To pass the time until light came through the window she silently listed them all. Brother's best friend, well-known outrageous flirt, the kind of guy who to her knowledge never stayed with anyone longer than five minutes. Firefighter.

The last one was the clincher really. Eddie was right. She didn't date firefighters. Had bloody good reason not to. Her childhood dream was reminding her all too clearly of that.

Nope. There was just no way. She'd have to weather whatever fad it was he was going through while she was under his roof. And then it would fade away and he could find another of his usual vacuous females to buy underwear for. He wouldn't be alone for long.

And she'd just go right on out and find someone who could get her just as hot. That shouldn't be a problem; she lived in the city, for cryin' out loud!

She had her own way in the morning and went to work. Though she did take the coward's route and leave before Shane got up to leave for the station.

Well, a girl had to do what a girl had to do.

At least work took her mind off things for a while. It was the busiest time of the year for a music distribution company, after all, thousands of discs making their way in and out of the door every day. And Lord knew she needed distraction from Shane now, as much as she did from her homeless state and the night-time meanderings of her over-active imagination.

The only thing that ruined her day was that no one seemed to have a sofa they could spare for a few weeks. That was what she got for being one of the last single ones in her group of friends. She was a year away from thirty and they were dropping like dominoes.

If Eddie had just lived alone instead of sharing with Shane there wouldn't have been a problem. Stupid brothers!

She would just have to avoid Shane. Heaven knew she'd managed it for this long. Well, avoided as in not given in to falling at his size elevens like every other single woman with a pulse, that was. He truly was almost as well known for his lack of commitment as he was for his looks, which helped.

Finn might not have been making an active search for a long-term partner, but she did believe in something more lasting than a few weeks' fun indoors, or outdoors, or hanging naked from a chandelier. And even if that kind of fun was *mighty* tempting, there was still the matter of his being her brother's best friend and a firefighter. She recited her morning list over and over to keep reminding herself. Brother's best friend, flirt, firefighter. Brother's best friend, flirt, firefighter...

She could get past basic carnal lust. She *could*.

But the minute she dragged her exhausted behind in through the door that evening and bravely sneaked upstairs, Shane was right in front of her, in the hallway, where she couldn't avoid him.

Coming out of the bathroom after his shower, wearing what looked like a hand towel…

She gasped and then forgot to breathe.

His head turned and he blinked slowly at her for a few seconds, studying her as if she were transparent. Then he grinned. 'Tough day at the office, babe?'

She swallowed hard and willed herself to focus on his blue eyes and not on the killer six-pack and the dark hair peeking along the towel edge. She could do it; she could hold a normal conversation with a pretty-much-naked Shane. She *could*.

'Erm…' She licked her lips. 'Great. Thanks.' She tilted her head and looked past his right ear. '*Busy.*'

Shane's grin grew and he stepped closer, leaning an arm out so he could rest his palm on the wall. 'Third of a year's business in one month and all that…'

'Uh-huh.' Oh, wow, did he smell good up close. He smelt of soap and shampoo and *testosterone*. Her mouth watered. But the fact he was so tempting and the fact that she couldn't string a sentence together started to get to her, so she turned her frustration at herself onto him. 'If you're into some weird naturalist thing you can bin it while I'm here.'

'There's nothing unnatural about doin' the things that come natural.'

She rolled her eyes at his words. 'It's stunning to me that you've stayed single.'

Shane's eyes seemed to glow at her. 'Maybe there's a reason for that. Maybe I need the right gal to pin me down. You have a think about it sure, and let me know if you can think of anyone who might keep me occupied long enough.' He pushed off the wall and turned around, turning his head to add, 'Bathroom's free.'

Her damn traitorous eyes watched as he walked down

the hallway. She watched the muscles in his back move, watched his taut thighs as he walked away. Even hoped, for a small second, that the hand bunching the corners of the tiny towel together might slip.

There was a hint of laughter in his voice as he rounded the corner. 'I think there's another one of these towels left.'

Oh, yeah. Because having just watched Mr. Eye Candy wandering around she was likely to squeeze her figure under anything less than a flipping beach towel! And with her hair in a turban and no make up on she'd just look great, wouldn't she? He'd really want to continue flirting with her then.

The smile started as a twitch at the corner of her mouth. Then it grew and grew until a bubble of laughter escaped. She clamped a hand over her mouth to stifle it.

If she was going to spend time in Shane's company, then he would have to learn that he couldn't wander around throwing his big sexy self in front of her every minute.

She would show him that she was just one of the guys. And yet gross him out with girly stuff at the same time.

The sooner he went back to treating her the way he always had, the sooner she could start doing the same thing with him. Because there wasn't really any point their being any other way.

Shane had spent a good portion of a nine-hour day shift thinking about Finn.

It really couldn't be helped. It was the underwear's fault. He might have been curious about her before, but now he was moving rapidly into the region of 'need to know'.

Especially after the fun he'd had flirting with her in the bar the night before.

He needed to know what she would look like in the

underwear they had bought. He needed to know whether
the slow looks he kept catching her giving him meant what
he thought they meant. He needed to know why it was he
needed to know with *her*. Why couldn't he have been so
damn interested in someone less complicated?

And he really wanted to know what would happen if he
went ahead and *made* things complicated.

He needed to know.

So he'd come up with a plan. In the last few hours of
his shift he had formulated a detailed plan to take advantage of the twist of fate that had thrown her under his roof.
Into the land where curiosity lived.

And, of course, he could keep her mind off her house
at the same time. Which was a considerate and thoughtful
thing to do, he reckoned. Even if he still laughed out loud
daily at what she'd done.

Planning was comfortable territory. It was a guy thing.
Shane had always felt comfortable with a good, well-
thought-out plan. Part of his training as a firefighter, he'd
guessed. In the service a guy knew how things worked,
where everyone should be and how each person's actions
could affect the overall picture. Guys stuck to the plan, to
a method of doing things to get results.

And, after all, if nothing else it would be a chance to get
to know her better, one on one. Something that he really
hadn't had much of a chance to do, seeing as he only ever
saw her when they had others around. One on one would
be good for a change.

Though where his night-time thoughts of one on one
had taken him recently had kind of veered off the path of
no involvement with his mate's sister. It had broken rules.
Which kinda made it even sexier.

He could hear her moving around the house when he went to his room. But by the time he was dressed he could hear running water in the bathroom. Which gave him time. Women didn't see baths as a way of getting clean. It was some kind of religious event to them.

So, with Eddie out for the evening with his girlfriend, he had time for step one of his plan: get her to relax and talk some. See if there were any more long looks to be had so he knew it wasn't just his furtive imagination. Though her reaction to him up close and almost naked in the hall had been encouraging.

While he'd walked away he'd even been tempted to throw his towel over one shoulder...

He started throwing together a supper and making the large open room 'comfortable'. He then lit a couple of candles that Eddie's girl had left behind. Women liked that kind of stuff.

In the half hour she took to reappear he had everything just about right: soft lighting, soft background music. He had even gone to the bother of setting places at the table in the kitchen rather than the usual balancing of plates on knees in front of the TV set that Eddie and he favoured when alone.

Pouring wine into two glasses as he heard her coming down the hallway, he turned with one in his hand and a smile on his face.

A smile that faded when he looked at her. 'What the—?'

'No wine for me thanks. A beer will be fine.' She walked past him and dug in the fridge for a bottle of her brother's favorite brand of beer, not bothering to look for a glass as she opened it. 'Bottoms up.'

Shane stared at her as she saluted him with the bottle,

then set it to her lips and drank a long gulp of the amber liquid. She raised an eyebrow at him. 'What?'

'What in hell is that stuff on your face?'

'Mashed-up avocado and honey, why?'

His eyes moved up for a second to the giant mussed-up ball of hair on her head, down over her green face to an oversized T-shirt with a lewd suggestion on the front that he recognized as Eddie's. Even the legs he liked so much were shrouded in beat-up sweat pants that Eddie would have worn to paint walls in and probably had, judging from the stains on them.

He blinked. 'No reason. I made us something to eat. But it can wait if you want to take that stuff off.'

Her shoulders shrugged beneath the voluminous shirt. 'It's good for the skin. I'm gonna go sit on the sofa and do my toes, so just yell when the food's ready, sure.'

Shane refused to shudder at the thought of what she might be doing with her toes. Instead he swallowed the contents of one redundant wineglass before turning around to find trays from the cupboard. His great plan wasn't going so good.

When he appeared with a tray she was hunched over her feet, giant wads of cotton wool separating her toes as she applied polish to each nail.

She glanced up at him, her eyes sparkling in the lamplight. 'You should have yelled.'

'You can walk with your feet like that?'

She smiled. 'Just about.'

As he set the tray on the coffee-table beside her his attention was momentarily caught by the TV screen. '*What* are you watching?'

'It's a makeover show where they show you all the surgery.'

He grimaced. 'Do we have to watch that while we eat?'

'You got a weak stomach?'

'I didn't used to, but that could do it.'

As he turned around he just caught the spark in her eyes before she turned her attention back to her feet. He knew that spark.

It was *mischief.*

She was up to something, wasn't she? And with a light-bulb moment he suddenly knew what it might be. It was a nice try. He'd give her that much.

She continued the charade. 'I think it's fascinating.'

'Do you now?'

She nodded. 'I'd have that done in a flash if I had the money.'

'You don't need it.'

'Sure I do; everyone has something they don't like about themselves.' She continued to focus on her toes.

'Like what?' Shane crossed his arms across his broad chest and raised a dark eyebrow at her, 'Show me and I'll let you know what I think.'

Yeah, right! Like she'd show him! That wasn't the point of this game at all. 'The whole thing about having parts of yourself you don't like is that you don't want them on display in the first place.'

'Okay, then.' He kept his expression deadpan even when he heard the edge to her voice. He was heading in a direction she'd been looking to avoid, unless he was very much mistaken. Directly into the kingdom of intimate in-formation.

If that was the case, then she damn well deserved whatever she got. Because she should have known better. It was *him* she was dealing with here. And she was messing up a plan he'd taken hours formulating, which meant there would be *consequences*.

'What would you change?'

Carefully taking her time to screw the lid firmly in place on the polish bottle, she then tilted her head to look up at him. 'Apart from losing about twenty pounds, you mean?'

'You're fine the way you are.'

'Yeah, right.'

'Not everyone likes the anorexic look.'

'Sure they don't, that's why every guy on the planet turns round to look at them as they walk past.'

He moved a little closer, unfolding his arms. 'Doesn't do it for me.'

She almost asked him what did, but wasn't sure she wanted to hear the answer. 'Well, you must get real hot at the thought of cellulite, then.'

'Haven't had much experience with it, I must say—' he smiled a slow, lazy smile '—but I'm always open to new experiences. So why don't you show me?'

Her eyes widened. This wasn't working the way she'd thought it would. In fact it was pretty much having the opposite effect. With a swift rethink she swung her legs off the sofa and pushed up onto her feet. 'I'm going to take this stuff off my face.'

'What about your food?' He stepped into her path.

'I just told you that losing weight isn't a bad idea. So skipping a meal or two might be a good place to start.'

'You don't need to lose weight.' His eyes made a slow study of her green face, then moved equally slowly down over her body. 'You curve in all the places a woman should curve. In *and* out.'

His eyes eventually locked with hers and gut instinct

told her she'd been caught. Her voice dropped a husky
octave as she warned him, 'Don't.'

'Don't what?'

'You know what.'

'Oh.' His eyes sparkled down at her, his mouth quirking.
'You mean this.'

Her traitorous feet froze to the ground as he encircled
her waist with his arms and pulled her body hard against
the length of his. She gulped, her voice barely a whisper.
'Please, Shane, be reasonable—'

'Well, since you asked so nicely…' He lowered his head,
and, regardless of the sticky avocado that smeared onto his
face, pressed his warm mouth to hers.

Her knees gave for a brief second. Oh, *c'mon*, this just
wasn't fair! No one had ever made her knees wobble
before. She had rugby players' knees, for crying out loud!
Nice sturdy knees that had held her upright perfectly well
for twenty-nine years.

He moved his mouth back and forth, adjusting to the
shape of her, discovering where they fitted best. Then, confidently, he deepened the kiss, running the tip of his tongue
over avocado at the edge of her mouth before pushing
against her lips and forcing her to taste the sweet concoction with him. *Payback time.*

An anguished moan escaped from deep in her throat.
Avocado had never tasted so good. Who knew it was an
aphrodisiac?

Large, competent hands moved against the material of
her huge shirt, smoothing it in against the small of her back,
moving around to shape the inward curve of her waist.

Her blood boiled, her abdomen twisting up almost painfully as spirals of desire had her squirming against him.

Heat thrummed through her veins, gathered at the apex of her thighs. Her body screaming: oh, yeah, *bring it on.*

She had to stop this, had to try and fight him off or, at the very least, struggle a little. She certainly needed to stop her traitorous mouth from joining in. Any second soon would be good.

Large hands moved again, slid down the outside of her thighs, around them, and then back up to curve her buttocks. Then his long fingers moved in a kneading motion before he drew her hard against his pelvis.

Her eyes shot open when she felt his hardening length push against the soft curve of her stomach. And she continued to stare, his face slowly coming into focus as he lifted his mouth from hers and gazed down at her with smoldering eyes.

He smiled slowly, stepped back, releasing her completely as one hand wiped avocado off his face. As he then carefully sucked each finger clean he looked her directly in the eye, his voice husky.

'You don't need to lose any weight, Finn. You fit me just fine.'

Well, hell. As he turned and walked calmly away she couldn't bring herself to say anything. She couldn't think beyond the fact that, having just had the hard length of him pressed so intimately against her, she wasn't convinced she could say the same thing to him.

Apparently the rumor about the size of men's feet wasn't entirely wrong.

CHAPTER FIVE

FINN spent most of the rest of the night tossing back and forth between cool sheets in a warm room. When she did catch any sleep it wasn't the deep, restful kind that would prepare her for another hectic day at work. Oh, no. It was that half-asleep, half-awake kind of time-wasting that allowed her troubled mind to make weird dreams out of her confused reality.

At least her dreams weren't about a man in a fire.

How dared Shane go and kiss her? Making things even more complicated than they were before!

How dared he make it a kiss that curled her toes and woke every nerve that had been asleep in her body.

Why couldn't he have had bad breath or been allergic to avocados? And why had he felt the need to make a pass at her when she'd done everything in her feminine handbook to appear unattractive?

But most of all damn the enormous lump of a man for making her furtive nocturnal imagination play with the idea of having worn avocado and honey *all over,* with having him smear it on slowly, and lick it off even slower. Did whipped cream go with avocado and honey?

By the time light was shining through the curtains she

was completely infuriated and mad at him. And by the time she came down for breakfast with her ultra-soft facial skin she was ready with a much-rehearsed put-down for *Mr* Shane Dwyer.

He didn't even have the courtesy to look up from his newspaper when she walked in.

'You're never doing that again; you hear me, you moron?'

'Doing what?'

'Oh, you know what.'

'If that's your attempt at predicting the future then you're way out.' He glanced up for a brief second. 'Whereas your horoscope for today says "red hot passion is headed your way".'

He smirked as he bit into his toast and continued with his mouth full. 'I'd say that was closer to the mark myself.'

'You…you…' she spluttered at him, angry heat rising on her cheeks '…you really are the most arrogant—'

'Now, Finn, *language*. Eddie said you weren't much of a morning person.'

She spoke aloud a word her mother probably didn't even know she knew. Would slap her silly for saying, even at *her* age. Irish mothers were famous that way.

He coughed as his toast went down the wrong way, then laughed. 'Man, did you ever get out of bed the wrong side this mornin'. Have some coffee, babe. Chill.'

'You just think this is hilarious, don't you?'

He continued smiling as he looked up at her stunned expression. Oh, she was angry all right. Angry, and, little did she know it, sexy as anything with it. Flushed cheeks, sparkling eyes, the rapid rise and fall of her breasts beneath her strait-laced jacket.

She'd be worth riling up every now and again.

For a brief second he wondered what she was wearing underneath her jacket. Was it something he'd picked, something lacy and brief and made to be removed?

His body was harder than a brick wall after one avocado-flavoured kiss. So hard that there'd barely be time to take that underwear off.

What was with that, then? What had happened to those rules down at the station? The rules he knew better than to break... In theory.

The very least he could have done, after years of playing the field, was choose to get all fired up with someone who wasn't going to fight him off tooth and nail or earn him a few black eyes along the way from his best mate.

Thing was, the chase was as erotic as hell.

'I think if you get this annoyed after one wee kiss then you're going to be fun to live with when we—'

'We *won't*! So you can just get that into your thick skull right this minute.'

'I think we will—' he nodded '—and I think you know we will too.'

'No, *we won't*.' She planted her hands on her hips and glared at him from the space between the kitchen and living room. 'Trust me.'

He took his time folding the newspaper before calmly setting it down on the table. Then, with his steady gaze fixed on her fiercely determined face, he stood up and took a step towards her.

When she moved back a step he merely quirked an eyebrow. 'We will, Finn. It's just a matter of when. This thing that's going on with us has been brewing a while and I think you know that as well as I do.' He took a step towards her, she took a step back. 'I wasn't the only one doing the kissing last night.'

She fired an answer back at him. 'Reflex.'

His eyebrows quirked in unison. 'What?'

Swinging a hand back and forth in front of her body, she avoided his eyes and explained, 'It was a knee-jerk thing, that's all.'

Dimples creased his cheeks as he laughed. 'Now, you see, a lesser guy would take that as an insult.'

'Well, thank goodness for your ego, then.'

'Maybe I should kiss you again to see who's right.'

'I already told you, you are *not* kissing me again!'

'All right.' He shrugged as her eyes shot to his in surprise. 'Next time you can kiss me. I like it when a woman takes the initiative. And not just at the kissing part, just so you know.'

'Shane—' She couldn't actually think what to say in reply to that while her mind painted some very dirty pictures of taking the initiative. There were several to pick from in her nocturnal imagination's personal version of *Nine and a Half Weeks*.

She glanced briefly at the fridge. 'Will you see some sense here? This really wouldn't be a good idea.'

'Is that you trying to convince me or you?'

'It's me talking sense!'

'Okay, then. Why not?'

Finn stared in astonishment as he crossed his arms across his chest. 'What do you mean, "why not"?'

'Why wouldn't it be a good idea?'

'Because.'

'Oh, well, *because*. I get it. That's that, then. Clear as mud when you put it that way.'

She swore again. 'Why is it I can't string a proper sentence together when you get like this?'

Shane shrugged again. 'Because I'm right?'

'I am not getting horizontally involved with you, Shane, so just deal with it. There are a million reasons why it wouldn't be the best plan in the world, and you know that.'

'I know you can date as many librarians, or whatever it is the guys you've been dating recently do, as you want to avoid me. But what we have here isn't going away. There's only one solution.'

'You think I've been dating—' she scowled when she almost said 'librarians' herself '—those guys to avoid *you*?'

'Haven't you?'

Her green eyes widened at the question. Had she? Was that what she'd been doing, avoiding Shane by dating the 'safer' options? Or someone just like Shane, someone hot and addictive?

Finn wouldn't allow herself to think that, even silently. Because if it was true it meant she had to think long and hard about the reasons *why* she would do that. And that was way more therapy than she had money to spend on.

Her chin rose. 'You're wrong.'

'Am I?' For the briefest moment he wondered if maybe he was. She seemed to have the ability to make him doubt his own powers of perception. Even with his vast experience.

But then his eyes dropped again to the rise and fall of her breasts, the flush at the base of her neck. And he smiled a slow smile. *Nah.* She wasn't this affected by him for no reason. 'I don't think so.'

He stepped forward again, she stepped back. Her feet moved swiftly from tiled floor to wooden. Many more steps of retreat and they'd be talking next door.

'If you're so immune to me, then how come you're so freaked out that I might touch you again?'

She stopped dead and raised her chin. 'I am not.'

It was getting tiring, especially after a night without much sleep. All that mental strain during the day planning a detailed plan of seduction and then a night spent making tents...

Shane sighed, running his hand back through his hair and searching the kitchen with his eyes for inspiration. When none appeared he looked back into green eyes filled with determination, taking in the stubborn rise of her chin along the way.

'There's no point in pretending this isn't here. It is. And we can argue about it all you like but it's not gonna change it.'

The truth of the words, so calmly spoken, made an angry retort die a death somewhere in the region of her throat. But there was one other truth that wouldn't change. 'I won't let myself fall for you.'

'You're taking this too seriously. I haven't asked you to marry me.'

The words were like a slap in the face. 'So we just roll about 'til one or the other of us gets bored? Is that how you see this going?'

'No!' His voice rose at her interpretation. 'Damn it, Finn, that's not what I meant.'

'But you see us doing something about—' she waved her hand back and forth between them '—this *thing* that's going on. You just don't see it as being anything too important? That's romantic. You're a real charmer.'

Ignoring the main part of what she was saying, he picked up on the one part that had come through clearly. 'At least you're admitting there *is* something going on.'

She flushed a fiery red. 'Answer the question, Shane.'

'Which was what?' He focused hard on forcing himself not to step forwards and shut her up the best way he knew how. She was shooting his great plan to win her over to hell in a handbag and all it did was add to his frustration.

He was a guy, for crying out loud. A guys' guy at that. He wasn't supposed to be good with words. And what did she expect from him so early on—wasn't just taking a chance to begin with a big enough step for her?

'You see me as some quick thrill, some sort of a challenge to you? Is that it?'

'No. That's not how I see you.' And it wasn't. He already cared about her. Something he didn't feel as if he had to tell her, as she should know by now! Hadn't he made it obvious?

'Then what is it you want?'

You. He knew the answer was just that simple. In his mind, anyway. And to him that was enough. Because he knew Finn McNeill. Had liked her more every time he'd met her or talked with her or played the verbal sparring game they were so good at. Then the liking had turned to curiosity and then to fascination.

It had only been a matter of time before the fascination had turned into something more. Anything more than that was a bigger step than he was ready to take. Never mind discuss.

He shook his head. 'How about we talk about this when you're in a better mood?'

'My mood is just fine, thanks.' Her eyes narrowed, 'You're the one that doesn't want to talk about this. Your solution is to just get physical and forget about the consequences.'

Shane could feel his temper rising. She was pushing harder than he'd ever let any woman push him before. And the worst part was, to a certain extent, she was right. It would be the easier option for him, had been before. To just give in to need and then walk away if he couldn't find it in himself to give anything more.

And with Finn it would all have to happen under cover of secrecy from their friends and family.

But that almost made it sordid. And she was worth more than that, wasn't she?

He tried to find a simpler solution. A starting point. 'Okay, then. Let's say I ask you out on a date. Just the two of us. Would you go?'

'No.' She stared him straight in the eye.

'Why not?'

'I don't have to give you a reason.'

He shook his head and sighed. 'No, you don't have to, you're right. But I think we've pretty much established that it wouldn't be because you don't fancy me.'

'If I do then it'll wear off.'

'You think?'

'I *know*.'

He shook his head again, 'Well, I hope you have better luck than I have. 'Cos wanting you would seem to be something I have no control over. And I have no idea what I'm supposed to do about findin' out what that means when you're being so bloody-minded.'

Finn gaped at him. It was quite a confession. And for a split second she actually considered thinking about it. Seriously considering an affair that would lead to major trouble all round. Was she insane?

Her first attempt at speaking failed on a croak that brought his gaze back to hers. So she cleared her throat and tried again.

'You want me that bad, Shane, then there's only one

thing you'd have to do to change my mind about seeing what might happen.'

'And that would be?'

'Quit the service. Quit the fire brigade and, I swear, we won't leave your room for a week. Then we'll just see what happens.'

'Now you're being ridiculous.'

She ignored the scowl on his face and ploughed on, frustration forcing the words out. 'If you were anyone else we wouldn't even be having this conversation. Eddie already told you that I don't date firefighters. *Full stop.*'

Eddie had. But Shane hadn't really paid much attention. Mainly because, at the time, it hadn't occurred to him that it was that important a detail. But now was a different matter.

Now he needed to know why. 'Why?'

'Because I won't end up like my mum did. That's why.'

The simple statement was said with wide eyes and flushed cheeks. Almost as if she hadn't really meant to say it out loud.

Then she gathered herself together, smoothing the front of her jacket with calm hands before she added with a short smirk, 'So that's the deal. Take it or leave it.'

Watching her leave, Shane knew she'd got him. Because she knew he wouldn't quit what he loved doing, wouldn't quit on the family.

Not for any woman.

CHAPTER SIX

EDDIE seemed oblivious to the tension in the house when he met Shane that evening.

'Hey, Shane, where's Finn at?'

She was hiding upstairs somewhere, he assumed. He'd heard the door slam on her return and had heard bath water running, but since then she'd been as silent as the grave.

And he didn't feel much like running up there to see what she was at. She could have drowned for all he knew.

Quit the fire brigade his ass!

'Upstairs somewhere.'

Eddie threw himself down on an armchair, one long leg swinging off an arm. 'How's she doing?'

'Fine.' He focused all his attention on the football match playing on the widescreen T.V. After a moment of silence he glanced over at Eddie's face. 'She seems to be coping just fine.'

Eddie nodded. 'She's a trooper.'

Oh yeah, she was *something*.

'You two getting on all right?'

The beer bottle in his hand froze halfway to his mouth. But Shane recovered quickly and raised it the rest of the way with barely a heartbeat of pause. 'Just dandy.'

Eddie laughed. 'You have a row already?'

'Not a row.' He shrugged. 'More of a difference of opinion.'

'That's my little sister, all right. She has differences of opinion with me all the time.'

Yeah, but Shane bet she'd never told him to leave his job before. It was on the tip of his tongue to open his mouth and say as much. But he knew it wasn't worth going there.

Thing was, under different circumstances Eddie would have been the one he'd have chatted to about it. Eddie would have understood how ridiculous her demand was, he would have laughed with him over a beer about women who tried to change men and why they felt they needed to do that. Eddie would have got it.

Whereas Finn evidently didn't.

She should have, though, coming from the background she came from. Not that that had helped her with fire safety of late.

Eddie bounded on in when his words were met with silence. 'What was it about?'

'Makeover shows.' It was the first answer that jumped into his head under pressure. 'She thinks she needs to go under the knife to fix her flaws.'

There was a burst of laughter from the chair. 'She'd better take that one up with Mum. It's her fault we all ended up the way we are. Hers and Dad's. Finn was always paranoid about her size. It's not easy being her height, and, *you know*, curvy.'

Shane tried to concentrate his gaze on the screen, though he had to blink a few times to get his mind off the word 'curvy'. Instead he focused his thoughts on something less sexual, attempting to keep his tone nonchalant. 'How *is* your mum?'

'Grand. She's been seeing some bank manager for a while. I think she likes the company.'

'She's happy, then?'

Eddie's eyes focused on Shane's profile. 'Course she is. Why the sudden concern?'

Turning his head towards his friend, he smiled. 'Can't I ask about my favourite girl?'

There was a burst of laughter. 'Yeah, twenty years younger and she says she could *be* your girl all right.'

Shane's eyes softened at the statement. Moira McNeill was a sweetheart who had 'adopted' him from the first day he'd been invited down with Eddie. He in turn flirted outrageously with her at every meeting. 'I could have been your stepdaddy.'

Eddie shuddered. 'Thanks for that image.'

'You're welcome, *sonny.*'

They fell into a companiable silence as the match reached half-time, then Shane stretched his long legs out in front of him and savoured another long mouthful of beer.

He mulled over the best way to broach the subject that had had him curious all day long, when he hadn't been mad enough to spit nails. Eventually he decided to just go for it.

'It must have been rough for her after your dad died.'

Eddie was silent for a few moments, his voice low when he answered. 'Yeah.'

'She's a gutsy lady.'

'Yes, she is.'

It was like getting blood from a stone. And Shane knew with a certainty borne of familiarity that he was flogging a dead donkey. He knew that Eddie and Finn had lost their dad when they were quite young. He knew that the man had been a fellow firefighter, but beyond that he didn't know a lot.

From Eddie's reaction to the questions, the answers weren't going to be found with him. Which meant he had no choice but to try finding out from Finn.

Which made Shane wish he didn't want to know.

'I'm gonna move in with Kathy.'

The words brought him out of his sombre thoughts. 'What?'

Avoiding the surprised eyes that looked in his direction, Eddie swung his leg off the side of the chair and sat with his elbows on his knees. 'Yeah. I've been thinkin' about it for a while but I didn't want to leave you in the lurch. What with Callum getting his own place and all.'

When Shane had bought his house it had been a little more than he'd planned on spending in month by month expenses. But with two mates from the station sharing the bills it had been a breeze. Callum had been the first to move on, buying his own place further outside the city. Which was why there'd been room for Finn lately.

'Don't worry about that. Moving in with Kathy is serious, though. You're sure?'

Eddie's face warmed. 'Yeah. Sure as I can be. We talked it over and it just feels right, you know?'

Actually he didn't. He'd never met anyone who had made him feel he could be with her twenty-four seven. But then he'd never spent time with a woman who got under his skin like—

He frowned.

Eddie misinterpreted the frown. 'I'm really sorry, Shane. I could leave a month's rent if it helps any.'

Shane schooled his features, grinned across at Eddie. 'Shut up. You don't need to leave anything; it's fine. I'll put a note on the board at work and someone will need a room. One would do. It's no big deal.'

Eddie seemed to relax. 'End of an era, though, isn't it?'

'Yeah, that it is. But it's not like you're planning on living under the thumb, is it?'

'Hell no.'

'Then nothing's changed beyond the fact I get complete control of the remote.' He waved the object back and forth between them with a wink.

There was a burst of laughter. 'Yeah, if you can wrestle it off Finn.'

A very vivid mental image of wrestling with Finn entered his head. Oh, they'd wrestle all right, he had enough information from their differences of opinion lately to know they could spark off each other. And after the few days she'd put him through he had every intention of torturing her long and slow.

'Hey, you should speak to her about staying on here for a while. All that insurance stuff can take months and you two get along most of the time.'

Now Eddie thought they should live together? That would be a new experience. One that, while he wrestled with her some, mightn't be all that bad. But if she really was serious about him quitting the service, they wouldn't exactly be perfect house-mates. 'I don't think that would work out.'

Eddie laughed. 'She'd cramp your style right enough.'

When Shane simply cocked a dark brow at him in response, he shrugged and continued, 'Anyway. Since I'm settling down I thought me and Kathy would throw a party to celebrate.'

'Good plan.' That was what the doctor ordered. A night of drunken pranks and the chance to bump into uncomplicated single women. 'You havin' it here?'

'No, over at Kathy's. She wants to play hostess.'

So much for drunken pranks. He grimaced. 'You mean a dinner party.'

'That was *her* plan. I have different ideas.' He pushed himself off the chair with a wicked grin. 'I even have a theme like we used to do when we had parties here. So I'm gonna skip upstairs here and invite Finn along too. She used to think those parties were a hoot.'

Shane reached his beer bottle to his lips as Eddie bounded upstairs. There was just no escaping from Finn, was there?

The bottle froze in mid-air for a second time. Hang on. Eddie was moving out. That meant he was going to be alone in the house with Finn. All alone.

There was no way he was quitting the fire brigade for her. But that didn't mean he couldn't work on her some more, wrestle with her until she saw he was right and she was wrong.

A slow smile worked its way across his mouth as he leaned back on the sofa and lifted his legs to cross them on the coffee-table in front of him. Shane Dwyer had never lost a fight before.

Finn McNeill had a heap of trouble headed her way.

If he kept looking at her like that she was going to scream. In the house she'd had to do major ducking and diving to avoid him, knowing it would take something miraculous to get them back to where they'd been before she'd given him her 'ultimatum'.

It had been a completely ridiculous suggestion. One she'd known there wasn't a bat's chance of him taking up. Because after all, Shane loved what he did and it wasn't as if Finn was known for being an irresistible sex goddess.

Not that she couldn't give as good as she got with the

right partner. If he had any idea the way her mind had been working of late…

But she *was* really missing the way they'd been before. The way they had been easy in each other's company, could have shared a few jokes and more than a little teasing. It had just been—simpler.

Now, every time she talked to someone or laughed along at a joke she could feel his eyes on her. The couple of times she attempted a sideways glance at him he would simply smile a slow smile and look her straight in the eye. And that simple glance was enough to run her blood faster through her veins, to have her heart stop for a beat and then quicken to compensate.

And the amount of effort she was putting into having a good time in front of him was getting exhausting.

'Finn, you're up,' Eddie's voice called from the sofa as he waved the slip of paper at her. 'Your name just came out of the tub.'

Great. Of all the adolescent ideas her brother had ever had for a party, this one was the most childish. Literally. She'd always hated his dumb themed parties.

'C'mon, Finn, don't go letting the family name down. Unless you'd prefer some nice dry paper and a match…'

With a scowl she made her way to the edge of the game mat. 'I hate you.'

'Nah, you love me really.' He put his hand back into the tub and drew another piece of paper, then laughed. 'Oh, this should be good.'

Finn glared at him as he laughed. There were at least a dozen names in that tub. There was just no way—

'Shane, my man!'

Aw, c'mon!

He walked slowly across the room, grinning as if he had known it would happen. 'This should be fun.'

Finn's chin rose. 'You're toast.'

He lifted his index finger and beckoned her forward, his eyes sparkling. 'Come on, then. Give it your best shot.'

Fine. He wanted to play, she'd play.

Ten minutes later she really didn't want to play any more. 'Watch it with the hands.'

'Oh, I'm watching, don't you worry.' Deep blue eyes gazed into hers up close and personal and then one of them closed in a lazy wink. 'I'm watching *really* closely.'

Finn aimed one of her patented 'drop dead' looks at him while he made his move. It was obviously in need of a battery change, though, because Shane just continued to grin at her, his face inches from her own.

He was just too damn close and the proximity was doing things to her it had no business doing. Boy, did she ever need to get out and find someone else who could do this to her. She was wound tight enough to commit murder.

In fact there was a likely candidate right in front of her. Did considering it make it premeditated?

'Finn, right foot green.'

She dragged her gaze away from his sparkling eyes and tried to twist her head around enough to find wherever green was. When she located a free circle she sighed. *Great.*

Shane's head dropped until he could see between his legs and then he laughed. The sound rumbled from low in his chest, vibrated the air in the small space between them, went straight down her neck and warmed her breasts, which went heavy and ached.

His head rose again and he looked into green eyes filled with resignation. 'Go for it, McNeill.'

'I look like a contortionist to you now?'

'I heard you'd started that yoga thing a while back and you *know* I'm ready for any of your hidden talents.' He tilted his head and added, 'But I'll bet you're thankful now that we didn't follow Eddie's suggestion of naked Twister…'

Finn blushed. Yet again. Damn it. This was so Eddie's fault. It had been *his* stroke of genius to run with the 'kids' games' themed party and it therefore followed that playing Twister was *his* fault too. They'd only just avoided any sort of nakedness because Finn had insisted that that didn't make it a 'kids' game' any more.

And now she was about to try and twist her body underneath Shane's, with an audience to boot. When she'd spent all of her efforts recently trying to avoid ending up in that exact position, *without* an audience.

Not that there wasn't enough room under there, even for her Rubenesque figure. He really did cast enough of a shadow to block out light over small European countries.

She ran her tongue along her lips as she tried to figure the best way of managing the move without quitting. Fionoula McNeill was no quitter, after all. She couldn't let him get the better of her. No way. She'd win this game if it killed her. Even if she was killed when Shane fell on her and crushed her to death.

All she had to do was focus on the game and less on his body so close to hers. Less on the familiar scent she was breathing in with each breath. And especially less on how every nerve ending in her body seemed to be boiling hot with the same awareness as standing next to open flames.

Simple really. She just needed to focus.

Shane felt a bolt of pure unadulterated heat run through him, blood running south, as the end of her pink tongue appeared. She even had the gall to curl it up slightly against her upper lip before she left it held between two rows of straight white teeth.

Her eyes narrowed in concentration, she swooshed her long hair to one side to see better, she made several slow blinks of her long lashes.

She knew how to entice without even trying. Could make the simplest of movements an invitation. And the urge to kiss her was so strong it almost floored him.

'I have somewhere to be next week, so are you moving or what?'

Finn caught the tense edge to his voice. Her head tilted and she batted her lashes at him. 'What's wrong—you feelin' a little shaky over there?' She pouted a bottom lip at him. 'Aw, you wanna quit, big guy?'

Shane's eyes glittered and he moved his face an inch closer, his breath fanning across her cheeks. 'Bring it on, babe. I can take it.'

Both their heads dropped as Finn made her move. She swung her right leg out in a half-circle over the edge of the slippery mat and then carefully rebalanced herself before slipping her bare foot under firstly her fingers, a careful swapping of fingers and thumb, and then under her thumb. Finally she stretched out and twisted her back so that her foot could reach the green circle underneath Shane.

With a triumphant smile she looked up into his face. 'Your move.'

She was practically underneath him, exactly where he'd wanted her of late. If there hadn't been an audience…

With his head tilted down, his eyes were within close viewing of her well-rounded breasts. Very close. And for a long while he just allowed himself to look. If they'd been playing naked Twister he would only have had to lean forward an inch and he could have placed his mouth right around—

'Ahem!' Eddie's voice sounded from beside them. 'That's my sister's assets you're ogling, pal.'

Shane glanced up at the audience on the long sofa, a thick wave of dark hair falling across his forehead. Deciding to brazen his way out of what had the potential to be a very dangerous place, he grinned. 'Can't say I'd noticed.'

'How can you miss them?'

'*Well—*'

'Would you two knock it off?'

They both looked back at Finn, Eddie lifting his shoulders and asking, 'What?'

'I'd prefer it if my breasts didn't become the subject of conversation tonight.'

Shane saw the colour rise in her cheeks and wondered if it was embarrassment or the exertion of staying 'in the game'. She was one hell of an opponent.

But she should have been used to ribbing about her 'attributes'; she'd certainly been getting it for years from Eddie and his friends, Shane included.

But now was different. There was an element of sexual tension that had never been acknowledged before and Shane knew it. It gave him a real kick, as it happened.

As to wondering why it was that way with Finn and never before with anyone else? Well, he wasn't so sure it mattered any more. The fact was it was there. And it was amazing.

His eyes skimmed down to her cleavage again. He'd never liked skinny women, maybe partly due to his own size. Nah, he didn't need some female who looked as if she might break in a brisk breeze. Someone a little sturdier, well rounded in all the right places, a woman who would fill his arms and occupy a more equal space in his bed. That was more to his liking. And Finn certainly filled all those criteria.

A glimpse of lace caught his eye. Was she wearing—?

'And *you* can just knock it on the head.'

Her voice brought his focus back to her face. Her flushed face, her wide eyes, the large dark pupils. He was looking desire straight in the eye. Oh, she might think she was putting up a fight. But she was *losing*.

He stared for a long moment and then smiled a slow, lazy smile. 'I believe you said it was my move.'

The dial was spun beside them. 'Left hand red, Shane.'

The smile remained as he craned his neck to look over her shoulder. With a dip of his head that brought his cheek to hers, he whispered, 'You just stay still, now; no fancy yoga moves to distract me. Let me do *all* the work.'

Finn swallowed hard to damp her dry mouth. She forced herself to breathe normally as he reached over her, stretching his hand towards the red circle. And then his groin brushed against her hip and her eyes widened.

He was getting *turned on* by this? Was there anything he didn't get turned on by?

Blue eyes rose again and she could see he knew. He knew she could feel him hard against her hip. He knew she knew he was turned on, knew that she knew it was because of her he was turned on. And he just went right on looking at her, almost challenging her with the slow blinking of his thick lashes.

Finn's fingers wobbled on the mat and his dimples deepened. 'Your move. *Babe.*'

CHAPTER SEVEN

FINN'S eyes narrowed at Shane's words, the sexual sugges-
tiveness in his voice.

Her move?

Well, he'd already given her the advantage in the latest
round of their game, hadn't he?

So she played her ace.

First of all she arched upwards, her shirt stretching at the
deep 'V' of her neckline. She saw his eyes drop, saw a pulse
beat against his temples before he looked back in her eyes.
Saw from his expression that he knew she was wearing one
of the concoctions of lace and dental floss he had favoured.

Then with a single blink of her eyes and a deliberately
slow licking of her lips she simply raised an eyebrow and
smiled. 'Indeed it is.'

She moved her hip up, then down, against his groin, just
the one time. And the result was swift. She heard his sharp
intake of breath and watched triumphantly as he wobbled.

Her smile grew as she watched him trying to exert some
self control. She watched a bead of perspiration appear on
his upper lip, the pupils in his eyes enlarging.

His voice dropped to a husky grumble, close to her face.
'You play dirty.'

'You'll never know…' Her mouth formed the whispered words with alluring deliberation.

That did it.

Those three simple words sent him over the edge and the muscles in his legs started to twitch. He wobbled, his feet began to slip on the mat. Hell, even he had his limits.

With a little swift thinking he managed to shift the bulk of his weight a split second before he landed on her, their bodies a tangle of limbs on the ground.

There was loud cheering and clapping in the background as Finn looked up into Shane's face with pure glee. '*Loser.*'

With her lush body entangled with his and his chest cushioned against her breasts he wasn't entirely sure that was true. In fact it was so close to his many night-time fantasies of late that it was almost a reward.

Though they were wearing less in his imagination.

'We really would have had more fun if we'd played it Eddie's way.'

'In your dreams.' She giggled the words at him, revelling in her victory.

Oh, yes, indeed.

Eddie called for the next names to be drawn from the Tupperware bowl, while Finn waited for Shane to be a gentleman and move so she could get up.

Yep, any second now he would move, leap to his feet and offer her a hand. That was what he would do. He had to know now he couldn't rule the roost with her, couldn't bully her into submission. And he had to know they still had an audience.

Any minute now.

He propped his elbow on the floor and rested his head on his hand. Then he studied her with an intense gaze.

Thinking about how to get up without hurting her. Obviously.

'You okay?'

Aha. Concern. The first step in ensuring she'd be fine when she stood up.

'I'm fine. Thanks.' She smiled.

A nod. 'Good.'

Finn blinked at him from the floor. He'd move now.

He blinked back.

She raised an eyebrow. It would be polite to return the favour and check he was okay she supposed. After all, it would be better to know he was capable of getting up on his own, mainly because she doubted she would be able to remove his sheer bulk alone.

'You?'

'Huh?' He smiled a small smile.

'You okay?'

'Oh, yeah. A hundred percent. Better than that, I'd say.'

She frowned when he said the words with an almost smug tone. She'd just won, for crying out loud! What did he have to be so pleased about? Her voice rose. 'Well could you move, then?'

'Yeah, move, Dwyer; we need the mat.'

She smiled smugly. 'See, they need the mat.'

'They can have it when the new players are here.'

Finn wanted badly to slap him. Instead she wriggled hard and pushed against his chest with her one free hand. 'Get off, you oaf.'

Shane stayed still, his voice dropping. 'You think you've won something here, don't you?'

'I know it comes as a big shock to you to lose at anything—' she wriggled harder, her eyes sparkling dangerously at him as she did so '—and this would be the second time in a few days for you, wouldn't it? Poor you.'

Shane nodded wisely. 'You may think I've lost—' he moved a tiny amount, so that his lower leg held her more firmly in place '—but I don't see it that way myself.'

She glared up at him, her breasts rising and falling rapidly. 'Oh, really.'

'Yes, really.'

'And how do you figure that one, then, genius?'

Lowering his head towards her, he whispered in a low grumble, 'Because firstly you wore the underwear I bought you.'

Finn felt a shiver run down her spine again, her breasts suddenly *very* confined within the lacy garment.

'And, secondly, payback for what you just did is going to be a heap of fun.'

When he moved back an inch to glance over his shoulder at their audience, Finn thought fast. She used his momentary lack of focus to kick hard and free herself. Then with a roll and a decidedly ungraceful scramble on the slippery mat she was on her feet and glaring down at him.

She raised her trembling hands to straighten first her hair and then her clothes, before letting his look of surprise lift a smile onto her face.

With a quick upward glance she put her acting skills into motion again, laughing loudly for the benefit of the masses. 'You're a jerk.'

He placed two large hands over his chest and flumped back onto the floor in mock pain. 'Ow.'

With another quick upward glance, this time directly into her brother's suspicious eyes, Finn rolled her own. 'He's such a jerk.'

'Yeah, well, we all know that.'

'I'm gonna get my stuff. I have work in the morning.' She smirked back at Shane. 'No, really, don't get up.'

'You're leaving?'

She glanced over at Eddie. 'I have work tomorrow. I'm gonna leave you boys to your games.'

Eddie glanced at Kathy beside him, leaned over to whisper something in her ear and then untangled his arm from around her shoulders before standing up. He jerked his head towards the hallway as he got closer to Finn. 'Could I have a quick word?'

Finn followed him through the crowd to the hall. 'Eddie, honestly, I have to go. We're hectic in work at the—'

'Yeah, yeah, third of a year. I know. It's just I needed to tell you something.'

'What's wrong?' She folded her arms across her breasts, her eyes narrowing in suspicion when he couldn't look her in the eye. 'What dumb stunt have you pulled this time?'

'You have so little faith in me.'

'No, I know you, that's all.'

He smiled back when she smiled affectionately at him, 'I'm gonna stay here from tonight.'

Finn's eyes widened. 'Right now this minute? I thought when you said you were moving that it would take a while.'

Eddie shrugged. 'Now that we've made the decision it seems stupid to wait. Life's too short.'

It was something they both understood only too well. Had known from earlier in life than had seemed fair at the time.

So Finn understood.

But it didn't make her feel any better about the fact that she was now stuck in Shane's house alone with Shane.

The look of uncertainty in her brother's eyes made her

see sense, though. She was being selfish, thinking only of herself and that just wasn't like her. Normally.

She reached a hand out for one of his and tangled their fingers before squeezing reassuringly. 'I'm happy for you; you know that, don't you?'

Eddie squeezed her hand in reply. Then he leaned down a little and looked her in the eye. 'You okay?'

'I'm fine.' She forced a bright smile for his benefit. 'Why wouldn't I be?'

'It can't be easy, what with losing the house and all.'

She smiled when he managed to mention her house without making a joke about how it had happened. 'No, that bit's not easy. But I'm fine, really.'

'Look, I just wanted to tell you not to worry. I know you do.' He lowered his head, gazing up into her eyes. 'I'm still gonna call after every shift like I always do.'

Her heart warmed, and it showed in her eyes. 'Thanks.'

'No problem.' Then his eyes narrowed. 'Will you be okay at Shane's?'

The question, coming from Eddie, caught her off guard. Just how much had he seen in the game they'd been playing not five minutes beforehand? The last thing she wanted to happen was for the situation she had with Shane to flow over into his relationship with Eddie. They'd been friends for ever. Like brothers almost.

Even if she herself had never quite managed to see him in the same light.

She was going to have to deal with her Shane problems alone. There was no way in hell she'd be held responsible for screwing up anything else.

Bright smile back in place, she squeezed the hand she held one last time before letting it go. 'I'll be fine, really.

It's only 'til after Christmas and then I'll have time to look for a place of my own again.'

Eddie leaned in and planted a kiss on her cheek. 'Well, if you ever need me to kick his butt, you just yell.'

'Oh, I will.' But she knew she never would. What was going on between them was between them, full stop.

All she had to do was decide exactly what she was going to do about dealing with Shane. A stark truth was forming in the front of her confused mind: he wasn't giving up.

He was on the sofa when she came down for a glass of water.

'Bad dream again?'

The sound of his deep voice in the dark room made her jump. 'You scared the life outta me! What are you doing down here in the dark?'

'Thinking.' He reached a hand out for the closest lamp and sent an arc of soft light around the room. 'I heard you calling out. Another five minutes and I was coming up.'

She was glad he hadn't. It had been worse this time and she had woken sobbing, had lain in the dark until the tears had subsided. To have woken like that with Shane beside her would have been too much. She didn't want to have to explain it to him, to have to try and psychoanalyse the dream to death on his insistence.

She pointed a limp arm in the direction of the kitchen. 'I just came down for a glass of water.'

'You want to talk about it?'

The soft tone accompanied with the warmth in blue eyes that looked like black pools in the dim light made her heart melt momentarily. He really could be a pretty damned tempting guy when he put his mind to it. 'Thanks. But I'm—'

'Fine?' His mouth quirked.

Finn smiled in response. 'Yeah.'

The clock on the kitchen wall ticked loudly, the noise magnified by the silence. Finn suddenly was conscious of her breathing, of how it had become more laboured and how her heart was beating erratically.

She shook her head. It was ridiculous to suddenly feel as shy as a teenager in his presence. She wasn't exactly a virgin who wouldn't know what to do with him when they finally…

Terrific. Now she'd mentally made the leap from 'never happen' to 'when'.

'What?'

She avoided his dark eyes, glancing around the room, 'Nothing.'

He continued watching as she turned on her heel and walked towards the kitchen. Then he took a breath. 'You can't avoid me for ever. We're alone in this house now.'

'I'm not avoiding you.'

There was a short burst of deep laughter. 'Liar.'

'I'm just giving you some space.'

'I don't need any space from you.'

'You need some time to get past all this…' she paused '…stuff.'

'You think that's all it would take?' He shook his head in frustration. 'You really don't get it, do you?'

Finn stood still while she heard him move off the sofa behind her. She should have had a sarcastic retort to his question, but she didn't. She should have turned round and gone back to her room, away from him. But she didn't.

She just stood still and waited until the air moved behind

her and his voice sounded close to her ear. 'This isn't some flash fire. It's been slow burning for a while.'

Her heart thudded painfully against her ribcage as a tingle of sensual awareness shuddered through her body. 'I can't get involved with you, Shane.'

'You've said. But I think it's not a case of can't.' His large hands rose and ran a whisper-like touch along the length of her bare arms, from elbows to wrists. 'It's more like won't, even though you know you want to. But all you're doing is delaying the inevitable.'

'You've decided to leave the service, then?'

The hands stilled, the fingers tightening round her wrists. 'You know I won't do that. You also know me well enough to know I won't quit that easy.'

She tried to wrench her arms free but he held on—not so tight a hold that it was painful. But tight enough to let her know he wasn't letting go. 'Stop it.'

With a tug he brought her body back against his. He spread his feet a little wider so he could support her weight, used his nose to push her hair back from her ear. He nuzzled against the curve of her lobe, and lowered his voice to a husky whisper when she didn't struggle. 'You don't want me to stop.'

Finn sighed, let her head fall back against his shoulder. She was too tired to fight him, hadn't had a deep, dreamless night's sleep since her pants had caught fire.

She'd just give in for a little minute and then she'd make him see sense. That there was nothing to be gained in a physical relationship with him and everything to lose.

The first touch of his heated mouth against her ear sent another shiver along her spine, sent heat to her core and waves of moisture below.

His tongue curved along the shell, traced the shape and then made a line along the sensitive line of her neck. It was heaven.

'You *really* don't want me to stop.'

Lord help her, she *really* didn't. She didn't pull away when he let her wrists go and splayed his hands over her hips. She didn't move when he kissed the curve between her neck and her shoulder or when he grazed his teeth in a light nip.

She did let out a low moan, though. And immediately his mouth curved into a smile against her skin.

He raised his head a half-inch as he moved splayed hands from her hips to her stomach, his fingers moving back and forth. 'That's it. You know you want this as much as I do. Quit fighting me, Finn.'

And she did know she wanted it. She was one great big walking hormone. All the signs were there: the muscles in her abdomen tensing while his hands moved up her ribcage, the heavy weight of her breasts begging for his touch, aching to be cupped by his long fingers.

There was no denying any of it.

The problem didn't lie with her body. It knew rightly what it wanted.

But thankfully her head was still in charge.

Finally finding the strength to move, she raised her hands and placed them over his, stilling the movement. Stopping the torture long enough for her to lift her head. 'I may want to. But, you're right, I won't.'

Shane froze behind her and she tensed, waiting for his anger. But it didn't come.

When he spoke, the words were still soft, still close enough to her ear for him to speak in a husky whisper. 'Explain why.'

The words froze in her throat and the inner battle between body, heart and mind was more painful than any physical pain she had ever experienced. Even the one time when she'd broken her arm as a kid.

The deep rumble came again. 'Tell me.'

'If I slept with you—' the deep breath she forced herself to take shuddered through her frame '—I'd be tied to you. That's what most women do, you see, they make the act an emotional thing.'

'Would that be so very bad?'

'Yes, it would—' her voice shook '—because if anything ever happened to you in your work, as a friend I'd feel pain. But bonded to you as a lover I might not survive it. I can't let myself get attached to you any more than I already am.'

His hands tightened, pressed in against her stomach, 'Nothing's going to happen to me.'

'You don't know that.'

'Finn—'

'You don't know—' she used her hands on his to prise them off her body '—and I just can't take that chance.'

She knew he would probably think she was being ridiculous, that she was overreacting to something that might never happen. But he hadn't been there before.

He hadn't been there when the car had pulled up at their front door. And the men in their dress uniforms had come to tell her mother that her husband was gone.

To tell all of them that Daddy would never walk through the door again or swing his small daughter up into his strong arms, holding her tight against his broad chest as he circled and circled until she was dizzy.

Shane hadn't been there when they had been told the

most important man in their lives would never come back. Because a fire had taken him away.

Finn could never put herself through that again. And she'd had childhood dreams to remind her.

With slow steps she turned and found the guts to look up at his face. She could see the confusion in his eyes, the frown of disagreement between his dark brows, the tense set of his mouth.

In a shaky voice she made the biggest confession of all. In an attempt to make him understand. 'You see, the thing is I already care about you too much, Shane. I have for a long time. I can't take a chance on maybe falling in love with you. And I don't think you'd want to take that chance either. Because you don't like that kind of involvement.'

She made it halfway up the stairs before he spoke. 'I get it better now. I don't agree with it all but I get it.'

Her steps faltered. 'Thank you.'

'Don't thank me, Finn. I didn't say I was giving up. I just understand better your reason for fighting so hard.'

'I won't change my mind.'

'And I won't go away. You can pretend that this will just fade out if you ignore it, but it won't. We're already different. You just need to remember I'm still here. *I'm still here.* And I'm not going to stop trying.'

CHAPTER EIGHT

'WHAT does that *mean* exactly?' Mel took a bite out of her sandwich and then deepened her voice. '*I'm still here…*'

'Would I ask you what you thought if I knew?'

'Sounds like a line from a movie.'

Finn was at a loss what to do next about Shane and talking to someone outside of it all had seemed like a good idea. So she had asked for a second opinion of sorts, feeling a weight was lifted that she could talk it out with *someone*.

Though her initial confession had been met with a good ten minutes of gloating…

'So?' She bit into her roll and rescued coleslaw from her chin with a napkin. 'You think I'm just being overly dramatic?'

'I think the dramatic part comes in when you think that getting down and dirty with him automatically means he's going to come to harm.' A shrug. 'Unless you're into some kinky stuff that might *do* him harm? Which might be fun, you must admit.'

Finn glared at her. 'You're supposed to be helping.'

'I am helping. You're just resisting my help.'

'You know I can't get involved with Shane and why. It just wouldn't work. Not with my luck. I'd spend the whole time waiting for something bad to happen to him and what kind of way is that to live? Even if it only lasted five minutes.'

'Oh, I bet it'd last way longer than five minutes. He's probably got enough moves to—' The warning glare stopped her. '*Okay*. But you're already involved with him, and that's the real problem here.'

Finn continued glaring. 'Still not helping.'

'Well, he's obviously not giving up without a fight and that should tell you something. Most guys who are knocked back that many times and are as successful with women as Shane Dwyer would just move on to the next in line. It's not like he would be lonely for long.'

Finn felt a flash of jealousy at the thought. Which brought a scowl to her face. She would not allow herself to be one of those women who played the 'if I can't have him no one can' game. Damn it.

She pushed her roll away, her appetite waning.

Mel leaned closer and patted her hand. 'Honey, don't beat yourself up so bad about this. I imagine he'd be pretty hard to resist. Why don't you just allow yourself a bit of a fling and get it out of both your systems? There's nothing to say it'll go any further than that.'

Finn laughed. 'Yeah, right. A bit of a fling. That'll help no end. Scratching an itch may work for him but it won't for me. I just want us back to where we were before.'

As if. Having had so much time to mull over the dilemma she knew all the facts. And one major fact was that he would never be just a fling for her.

Shane Dwyer was the kind of guy women went weak at the knees over; his very profession immediately trans-formed him into hero material in an age where it was tough to find the shiny-clothed guys on horses. Certainly in the city anyway. Finn knew. She'd dated a few of the less shiny ones. And dozens of rusty ones.

Add to that the fact that Shane was strong, in character as well as body, that he cared, probably felt things deeper than he ever showed. All things pointed to the kind of guy that a female with half a brain would want for a long, long time. Not just a few weeks of mind-blowing sensual pleasure.

And Finn just knew, low down in the places *where* a grown woman's body knew, there *would* be satisfaction. Deep, rippling, toe-curling, crying-out-loud—

'Finn?'

'Sorry.' She shook her head to clear the images and checked her watch to hide her flushed cheeks. 'I gotta get back.'

Mel looked at her own watch. 'You've only had a half-hour.'

'We're manic. You know the music business and Christmas…'

'Yeah, you've mentioned it every year since you went to work there. Third of a year's business in one month, yada, yada, yada…' She tilted her head from side to side with each 'yada', then stopped to waggle a finger. 'But I still think that geek of a boss of yours could have given you time off since your house *burned down*!'

Finn sighed. 'I can hardly say much when it was me that caused it, can I? And, anyway, I need this job more than ever now. And at least while I'm flat out at work I'm not having to sit on a sofa watching TV with flipping Shane.'

'Or doing anything else with him, for that matter.'

She rolled her eyes. 'It's more exhausting being there than it is being in work.' After folding her roll back into its wrapping, she pushed it into her large bag for later. 'I just need to get through the next two and a half weeks and then I can try and find somewhere else to live.'

Mel grimaced. 'Have I mentioned in the last five minutes how bad I feel about there not being any space where I am now? We're on top of each other in that flat as it is. Are you quite sure you can't just go home to your mum's?'

Finn shook her head. 'It's a two-hour commute either way, and that's four hours I just don't have at this time of year.' One hand reached out and patted Mel's sleeve as she stood up. 'It's not your fault, hon, don't worry about it. I'll be home for Christmas soon anyway.'

Her friend smiled, a twinkle in her eyes. 'And safe?'

'Ha, ha.' She flung the strap of her bag over her shoulder, planted a kiss on Mel's cheek and turned to leave.

'Finn.'

The hand on her arm stopped her. 'What?'

'Just have a wee think about why he's chasing you so hard? It might be he sees you as more than an itch.'

Finn laughed a short burst of laughter. 'Mr Love-'em-an'-leave-'em? I think not.'

She squeezed Mel's hand and then turned to leave again.

She got as far as the door before her name sounded once more. 'Hey, Finn?'

'Yes?' She looked over her shoulder as her hand pushed open the glass door of the sandwich bar. 'What?'

'Just remember—' Mel winked across at her and added in a 'Terminator' voice '—*he'll still be there.*'

Laughing despite the fact it really wasn't funny, she pushed out into the crowded street and drew the lapels of her coat up against her face.

The early December wind was crisp and whistling, stinging against her cheeks and tossing her hair into her eyes. So it took several brisk steps with her face tucked into her coat before she could hear her mobile ringing.

Jostling past a couple of Christmas shoppers, she leaned against a shop window and fished it out of her coat pocket, glancing briefly at the name on screen before she answered with a frown. It was too early for an end of shift call. 'Hi, Eddie. What's up?'

She could barely hear him. 'You'll have to speak louder, I'm in the middle of town.'

'Just wanted to let you know we were okay before you heard any news.'

'What news?' Her half eaten sandwich churned in her stomach. 'What happened?'

'There was a house fire early in our shift. We got the call out.'

'What happened, Eddie?' It was Eddie calling so she knew he was okay. But she also knew that it was one of the days when Shane and Eddie worked a shift together. 'Was someone hurt?'

'It was hairy. But everyone's okay.'

'Shane——?' She tried to control the edge of panic in her voice. 'Is he with you?'

'No. But he's fine.'

Fine? Finn knew only too well how useless the word could be in describing how a person really was. '*What* happened?'

'It was a family. Couple of them had close calls. I just didn't want you to worry in case it made the news.'

The call was currently worrying her more than the news would have done.

Eddie paused, his voice more serious than usual. 'Look, sis, when we get a call out like this one, me and Shane normally talk it through that night. But I don't live there any more. You do, and I just wanted to give you the heads up. Just in case. Though you know he's not much of a talker usually.'

'You want *me* to talk him through it?'

'You're the right kind of person. You get it, Finn. You know better than most.' He paused again. 'And, like I said, it was hairy for a bit.'

'Busy day?' Shane didn't turn round when she got home late that evening after another hectic day in work. A day when she'd made more mistakes than usual with orders, distracted by what was to come.

She didn't know if she would find him a depressed, slumped heap, drinking his day into oblivion, or a cheery figure trying to pretend he hadn't had a tougher day than most of the population.

But he was neither.

His voice was steady and he just kept on making dinner at a bench in the kitchen, slicing vegetables with even knife strokes. To anyone else it would have seemed nothing was out of the ordinary.

Finn wasn't anyone else. She knew him well enough to see tension in the set of his shoulders, to recognize the overly calm tone to his voice as false.

'Not as busy as yours.'

'Just some more evidence for your reason not to get involved with me, I s'pose.'

She ignored the jibe, even though for a brief second she wanted to say, 'Fine, then,' and leave him to it. It would have been the easier option. But Finn had always been a bit too bloody-minded for 'easy'. 'Eddie said it was hairy.'

'There were moments.'

'You want to tell me about it?'

His burst of laughter was harsh. 'Not so much.'

'Maybe it would help to talk.'

'You're a therapist now?' He glanced over his shoulder, then slowly turned around and faced her.

She stared with wide eyes. 'Oh, my God.'

Wide shoulders merely shrugged in response to her gasp. 'It's just a few bruises.'

It was way more than a few bruises. He looked as if he'd been run over by a bus.

His face. His gorgeous face was covered down one side with cuts and angry swelling, his right eye half closed over, his cheekbone red and angry. Only his mouth seemed to have escaped.

Forcing her feet forwards, she asked in a small voice, 'What happened?'

His shoulders shrugged again. 'Some stuff fell.'

The words made her heavy feet stop while an over-played scene from her dreams flashed in front of her. 'Did the roof fall in?'

Shane frowned in confusion. 'No, the roof didn't fall in. Who said it did?'

She shook her head. 'No one.'

'That overactive imagination of yours again.'

Maybe so. But she didn't stop to think it over because she couldn't stop looking at his face, her eyes moving over every scrape.

He managed a small smile. 'I'm not scarred for life.'

Finn blinked and swallowed hard. Then she looked away. It didn't matter what had fallen, didn't matter to her whether the bruising would be gone in a day or a week.

Because the damage was already done. She'd already been forced to look her fears in the face.

But if she had thought holding herself back from sleeping with him would make it any less painful to her if he got hurt, then she'd been wrong. Very wrong.

The only thing she wanted to do was step forwards and fling herself into his arms. To have him hold her tight, to reassure her that he was still there, that he was safe.

Anger rose inside her, burning in her stomach like acid. *Son-of-a—*

She spun on her heel and ran back through the living room and up the stairs, his voice sounding out behind her.

'*Finn*! Finn, wait a minute!'

His heavier feet sounded on the stairs, giving chase. 'Stop, would you?'

She was almost in the safety of her room when his hand grasped her shoulder and swung her round. He then pushed her hard, her back hitting the wall. 'Look at me.'

Her eyes stayed fixed on the rise and fall of his broad chest, on the heavy breathing that was so real and reassuring.

'*Look at me*!'

With slow blinking she gradually raised her eyes. It was when she could see his face again that tears came. Hot, angry, frustrated tears, blurring the view of what she already knew was there.

'No, don't do that.' He raised his free hand and brushed her hair back from her cheek with tenderness that only made her cry more. 'I'm fine.'

She jerked her face from his touch. 'Don't say fine. You're not *fine*.'

He scowled at her. 'Yeah, I am.'

Green eyes locked with blue. Finn was angry. So, so

angry. He'd just given her all the proof she needed that she was right not to get any more involved with him. But he'd also just shown her that she already cared what happened to him, that, no matter how she tried avoiding him, he was already entangled in her life.

And the fact that one thing was so conflicted with another made her mad. Mad at *him*. Mad that he had made her cry in front of him so that he knew she cared without her even having to say so out loud.

Thick, dark lashes blinked slowly at her, his hand rising again, this time to her neck where his fingers curled into her hair, cupping the back of her head. He stared, a steady gaze that felt as if it could see through to her soul. And there was a tenderness there that made her mind up for her.

Without thinking any further, she grasped handfuls of his shirt and pulled herself forwards, forced her mouth onto his.

The last tears rolled silently off her lashes as she felt him tense against her, then he groaned and matched her move for move, their heads moving frantically from side to side. His long fingers moved against the back of her neck, his other hand snaking around her waist to hold her so tight she could barely breathe.

Somewhere in the back of her mind there was a momentary sense of panic. A 'what am I doing?' But while she had her fists tangled into his shirt and her tongue tangling with his it was tough to think much beyond wanting his weight on her, wanting to feel his skin on hers.

Releasing the tight grip she had on the material and overwhelmed by the combined heat of their mouths, she let her hands drop to the bottom of his shirt. Her knuckles grazed against the bulge of his erection beneath the shirt edge and she smiled against his mouth. This was all the reality she was interested in.

Tomorrow and its repercussions could wait.

Her fingertips found where the shirt edges met at the first button and she gripped again. Gripped and then tugged with all her strength, popping buttons that pinged off the wall behind her and clattered onto the wooden floor. It took two tugs. And then he was hers to touch. So she did, savouring the sensation of taut, warm skin.

Flattening her hands against the flatness of his abdomen, she smoothed her palms up while her fingertips dipped and rose over each of his ribs, turning her wrists as she swept over his nipples to his broad shoulders where she pushed the shirt back, then down along his arms.

Shane dropped his hands from her long enough to give his arms one shake so the shirt hit the ground at his feet. Then his hands were on her, undoing the buttons on her jacket with infinitely more finesse than she'd used on him. Finesse that he then used on the tiny buttons of her blouse, each one undone with a deliberate slowness that drove her insane.

So she helped him. Tore her hands from his skin to struggle out of her clothes, pushed off the wall to reach for the clasp of her lace bra, kicked her heels off her feet so that she had to rise up on her toes to keep kissing him.

His hands closed over hers behind her back. Squeezed once, removed them from the clasp. Then he tore his mouth from hers and looked into her eyes, his head still tilted. He didn't speak, didn't say a single word as he undid the clasp, smoothed his roughened fingertips up along her shoulder blades to slide the lace straps slowly from her arms. As he eased his body back an inch, eyes steady, the wisp of material slithered off her breasts and whispered against her stomach before it joined his shirt.

Then he leaned his head back, looked down at her full breasts, raised his thick lashes to look at her. And she knew instinctively he was giving her a second to think about what was happening.

A second that, had it been any longer, she might sensibly have used to step away.

But when his hands were on her breasts, cupping their weight and teasing her taut nipples with his fingers, there wasn't any room for thinking sensibly.

Finn flopped back against the wall, her head tilting back, lips parting as she surrendered to sensation. Her hand fumbled for the door handle beside her, almost of its own accord. But when she found it and opened the door to her room her eyes opened and she looked at him as he looked through the gap.

He looked back at her again.

Her eyes flickered over his face, from the thick dark wave of hair that fell across his forehead, past equally dark eyebrows to the sparkling blue of his eyes. Past the cuts and bruising on one side to the smooth flushed skin on the other. To the sensual sweep of his mouth with its fuller lower lip. There was no going back.

While she had studied him it was almost as if time had slowed. But by the time they were moving into her room everything sped up. Clothes hit the ground, mouths touched and seared and parted. Then Finn's knees hit the back of the bed and they tumbled back.

It occurred to her that he was wearing more than her. His hard length pushing against her thigh beneath the soft layer of his cotton boxers. She rolled over, straddling his hips, her breasts crushing against the coarse hair on his chest as she asked in a husky voice, 'Protection?'

Shane laughed a deep, purely sexual laugh that teased the hair that fell against her nipples and sent waves of wet warmth to her core. 'Across the hall.'

Finn froze, her eyes widening as she looked down at him. 'You're kidding me.'

'Nope.' He shook his head.

She blinked at him for several long moments. But when he smiled, his dimples flashing, then grimaced slightly at the pain it caused his cheek, she couldn't help but laugh too. 'I s'pose I have to go get it?'

'We'll both go. Sit up.' He continued smiling when her eyebrows rose. 'Sit up.'

So she did, sighing breathily as his erect penis settled between her legs.

Shane groaned. 'If we don't get a move on I'm not going to last 'til we get across the hall.'

And with that he pushed up on his elbows, wrapped his arms around her waist and pushed their bodies to the end of the bed.

Finn gasped when he pushed upwards. 'What do you think you're doing? You'll break your back.'

'Shut up and wrap your legs around me.'

'You can't—'

He was already on his feet so she had no choice but to do as she was bid. She wrapped her legs around his waist, gasping again as he hoisted her up so that her breasts were once again grazed over his chest hair. It was too, too good and she'd honestly never been so turned on in her entire life. But then she'd never had anyone carry her to their bed before. She'd never actually believed that anyone would be strong enough to do that. And it was the sexiest thing in the world.

They were in his room fast. He deposited her unceremoniously on his bed, yanked open his dresser drawer, tore open the foil packet with his teeth while his free hand pulled his boxers off and then he was on her.

She opened her legs with barely a hint of a touch from his hand on her knee; her eyes flickered closed again.

'Look at me.'

Her eyes opened and she looked up at his face, his body poised above her. 'Don't close your eyes. I want to see what you're feeling.'

It was the most difficult thing anyone had ever asked of her. More intimate than anything she'd ever experienced and for a moment it was the most frightening.

What was she doing?

But as the thick length of him slid into her with one smooth, practised stroke, all thinking stopped.

Finn's breasts rose and fell in deep staggering breaths. There were no words. Nothing beyond the sensation of being so completely filled, nothing beyond the ache low in her abdomen.

Then he moved, slid out until he almost left her, pushed back in to fill her again. His eyes locked on hers.

Her breathing got faster, the knot in her abdomen got tighter, his smooth strokes got faster and harder. And the urge to close her eyes and get lost in sensation was overwhelming.

'*Don't-close-your-eyes.*'

Her body arched up to his, the knot bunched her stomach muscles tight and then her release came, shattering her nerves and rippling out in spirals across her body. And her cries echoed around the room.

Through the haze of her pleasure she saw his brow crease, saw the dark pupils in his eyes enlarge until she could barely see the blue. Then he moaned—his body spent in ecstacy.

Finn stared up at him in wonder as he smiled a slow, sensual smile down at her.

Oh, *now* she'd gone and done it, hadn't she?

CHAPTER NINE

SHANE wasn't sure how he knew something had changed. But he knew.

At one point, when they'd been in the hall, it had crossed his mind that he should have stopped what was happening. For Finn to have changed her mind so suddenly should have shouted a warning note to him. He should have taken a moment to slow down and get her to talk things through. Even though talking things through wasn't really his forte.

But he'd wanted her for so long, had fanatisized so much, that having his desires presented to him had been too damn hard to resist.

It had been when he'd been buried deep inside her for the first time that the magnitude of what had been happening had hit him.

He'd never felt so connected to someone in his entire life. Not physically, not emotionally and most certainly not so strong a combination of the two that it had rocked him to his core.

He couldn't ever remember having felt so deep a sense of fear. Even when fire had been burning around him or when he'd known that lives were at risk.

The only thing that had kept that fear at bay had been

his body's need for completion. And even that had been way more than he'd ever experienced.

But before he could take the time to think it all through he knew something changed in her.

Then her expressive eyes closed before he could search them for answers.

Their bodies still joined, he leaned down and brushed a light kiss across her swollen lips, his voice a whisper. 'Don't shut me out.'

Her breasts rose and fell in a shuddering breath. 'I didn't exactly plan for this to happen.'

'I know you didn't. But it did.'

'Boy, did it.'

He laughed a low laugh. 'Yeah.'

Her eyes flickered open and she studied his face for a long moment. 'It doesn't change anything.'

It didn't? How did it not? He'd just had the most mind-shattering sensual experience of his life and she was telling him it didn't change anything? What was it, then—sympathy sex?

'Oh, really?'

'It can't.'

Maybe not from where she lay. 'We just made love. I'd say that changes things plenty.'

Her tongue ran nervously over her lips. 'I guess you were right—this was going to happen at some point. And it was—'

'Yes, *it was*.'

'But you got hurt today.'

'And that confirms your reasons for not getting involved with me.'

'Yes.' The expression on her face seemed to soften,

probably because she believed that his understanding meant he agreed with her. 'It does.'

Shane studied her for a long moment, then moved, breaking the bond their bodies had to adjust his weight so that his legs stayed tangled with hers. With one hand he reached for the edge of the bedcovers and drew them over their torsos.

Then he propped his hand on an elbow so his face was still close to hers and raised a hand to brush damp tendrils of hair from her cheek. 'And the first thing you felt you had to do when you had your fears confirmed was to get closer to me. You say one thing but your body says another.'

Finn didn't look at him, her gaze fixed on the ceiling.

'What happened today wasn't that big a deal. Really.'

He waited while she carefully considered what he'd just said. Then her face turned towards his. 'So what fell?'

Shane shook his head. 'You don't need to know that.'

'I want to know.'

'I already said it wasn't a big deal.'

But Finn refused to be deterred. 'You talk to Eddie about this kind of thing after it happens.'

'I'm not lying naked in bed with Eddie.'

'Why don't you want to talk about it if it was no big deal?'

The question made him think some. He could make an excuse or just try showing her again what kind of a connection they already had. But he felt she needed a little honesty if they were ever going to head in the direction he would like them to try heading.

'I guess I'm a wee bit worried that if I talk to you, you might use it as evidence for the prosecution in the case of McNeill v. Dwyer.'

From the flash of guilt that crossed her eyes he knew he was right.

'Okay.'

'That's what I thought.'

'No, I mean okay, you have a point. I don't mean okay, we don't have to talk about it. I want to hear it.'

'Why?' He looked her straight in the eye as he asked.

But with a flicker of her lashes she looked away and hid from him. Her naked shoulders shrugged. 'I think I need to hear some of what you do to understand it. You're telling me it was no big deal, your face tells me different and I want to know. You can't just tell me it was no big deal and then not tell me the details. All that does is let my imagination go wild and that has to be worse than "no big deal".'

She paused for breath. 'So, let me make up my own mind.'

'It's not like this every day. Most days it's just sitting around checking equipment, cleaning up and playing cards.'

'But some days it's not.'

'Some days it's not.' He nodded slowly.

'It's those days I need to hear about.'

It didn't make any sense to him. How could she be so determined that it was his job that held them apart and yet, when they finally had a moment where they could communicate, want to talk about that job? And the worst-case scenarios of that job to boot?

'Eddie must talk to you about it sometimes?'

She glanced up at him from underneath long lashes. 'Not really. He'll say things like "It was a rough one", or, "We had a bad day today", but he never goes into details. It's a firefighter thing, right?'

Shane smiled, 'Yeah, I guess it is.'

'Well, break it, then.'

'Talking about it isn't going to make you run screaming from this room?'

She thought that over for another minute, the tip of her tongue damping her lips again. 'You said it was no big deal.'

With a shake of his head he realized she had him. It was disconcerting having someone who could out-think him. Another first to add to the list of firsts he was experiencing.

Shane knew that what he told her might well enforce her fears about what he did for a living, but by not talking to her he would be closing a door on her. Which he didn't want to do.

He'd never talked to a woman about his job, not in any great detail. Maybe simply because he'd never met a woman he wanted to share that much with. The things that made him who he was. It was an intimacy he'd never felt the need to share. Well, there had to be a first time, he guessed.

'They didn't have a smoke alarm.'

Her eyes fixed on his.

He frowned. 'Anyone with a family that doesn't have a smoke alarm is a bloody fool.'

'Were there kids?'

A sharp nod. 'Yes.'

'Did they—?'

'We got them. But we had a hell of a time finding them in the smoke.'

She was blinking at him and he wondered what she was thinking, what pictures were forming in her mind. She was a smart girl, after all.

Doing his best to keep his voice calm, he rhymed off the order things had happened in. 'It was a house fire, persons reported. When we got there the bottom floor was pretty much a goner, the smoke upstairs was thick. And it's the smoke that does the damage. Everyone thinks that the fire does it but it's the smoke that's the real killer. Me and

Eddie were on one of the B.A. crews, so we put on tanks and went in.'

She continued to blink, her eyes flickering to his bruising. 'What happened?'

'There were two kids left inside at the back of the house. Callum and Mick found the first one on the floor beside his bed but we couldn't find the little girl.' He took a moment to study her face. 'You okay with this?'

She nodded. 'Go on.'

'I could hear her crying. She'd hidden in a laundry basket. Apparently she spends a load of time hiding and it's one of her favourite places. Eddie got her and I followed them down the stairs when the last three gave and I fell against the banisters. Knocked my face mask up and that was that. Everyone was okay. The parents and the boy had some smoke inhalation, the dad had some minor burns.'

'And the girl?'

Shane smiled softly. 'Not a mark. And the damp towels in the laundry basket helped her avoid the smoke.'

Finn stayed silent, her eyes locked on his. Then she asked, 'Do you get scared when you go into something like that?'

'You don't get time to get scared. It's a job. You know what you have to do and you focus on that. Then you get out.'

'Even when you felt the stairs falling?'

'I was nearly at the bottom. They'd have got me if I was hurt that bad. Relying on each other the way we all do is the most important part.'

He listened to her saying nothing at all for as long as he could stand it. 'You wanted to talk. That's a two-way thing, I've been told.'

'I just don't understand how you can do it. How you can

walk into places like that and not be scared. How you can risk your life like that.'

'I told you, it's not like that every day.' She didn't look convinced so he kept talking. 'And it's not just for the people I don't know, Finn. It's for the guys I work with. I couldn't be as close to them all as I am and sit at home knowing they were doing the job without me.'

'They're like a family to you.' She stated the obvious.

'You know they are.'

She looked away from him. But not quickly enough for him not to see her eyes shimmer for the second time in one night. He wrapped an arm over her waist, held her in place so she couldn't get away from him. 'You know what I do, Finn. I know you're worried and I know you care. Or you wouldn't be lying here.'

'I've never said I didn't care.'

'Then stop trying to run away every five minutes.'

Her hand settled on his on her stomach. She focused her attention on them, on the differences in size between his and hers. It was a powerful reminder of the difference between the male and the female and she was very aware of her own femininity while she was lying against the hard length of him.

Normally she felt like Goliath most of the time. Her height and her curved figure made her stand out in a society that seemed to be made up of five-foot-six women with sylph-like figures.

But Shane was so large, so broad, so muscled, that she felt small and vulnerable beside him. It was a nice sensation. Better than nice. It would be easy to just get lost in him as she had not so long ago, to give in to her body and try and shut out her mind. She just wasn't so sure she was as brave as him.

'Tell me what you're thinking.'

The deep voice so close to her ear sent shivers of aware-ness over the body newly educated to what he could do.

'What do you want from me?'

She felt him go still beside her but couldn't bring herself to look at his face.

'I guess I want you to give this a try.'

'Why?'

He went silent, and then it sounded as if he had to force the words through. 'Because I care about you too.'

The simplicity of it tore a hole in her chest. 'I don't know if I can—'

'*No*, you don't know. But there's only one way to find out, isn't there?'

CHAPTER TEN

SHANE started a delicious form of torment with phone calls the next day. Phone calls that started with questions about what Finn was doing and how her day was going and then rapidly progressed to debating what underwear she was wearing.

Then he would finish the conversation by telling her where he wanted to touch her, what it would feel like to have his hands on her when she got back to the house.

By the third call she was on fire and pretty sure everyone in her workplace knew what she was thinking about while she faltered in her telesales calls.

It led her to wonder at what it was about him that had her so hot. At her age in the current millennium, it wasn't as if she were some doe-eyed virgin, but she'd never met anyone who could do the things to her imagination that he could.

Having thought that over, she smiled when she inwardly admitted that no one had ever actually phoned her at her work to talk to her the way he had. There was just something so damn sexy about that. How could the 'librarian' types that preceded him possibly hope to compete?

Not that she wasn't sure that, somewhere in the world,

there was bound to be a 'librarian' type with just as dirty a mind. She just hadn't met him, was all.

Though in amongst all the sexual distraction, there were still doubts. Sex really wasn't the problem. If she hadn't known that from their first frantic encounter, then she would sure have known it from the slow deliberation of their second.

She hadn't been able to answer him with words. Having wanted to talk, she just hadn't been able to find any more words. So she'd done what she'd allowed herself to do the first time, she'd reached out for him. It seemed to be the one thing she felt she was in control of. An old-fashioned feminine thing that a woman had when she knew a man wanted her. But even that wasn't enough to take away the fear.

Surely walking away from him, even now when it would hurt so much, had to be better than having him taken from her later down the line?

By four she found herself doing something she'd never done at work before. Clock-watching.

It was just a shame her boss saw her doing it.

'You in a hurry to be somewhere?'

Heat rushed over her cheeks. 'No, I'm just mad keen to have these orders ready for the courier.'

'Well, it's as well. We have a shipment from England coming in late. So it's all hands on deck tonight.'

Finn sighed when he was out of earshot. Great. It wasn't that she wasn't used to working all the extra hours at any particular time of year; it wasn't that she didn't get paid decent overtime rates and a fairly generous Christmas bonus at the end of it—the latter two subjects things that she needed more than she ever had before.

It was just that for the first time in several years of

Christmas overtime she had somewhere else she would rather be. As if her time with Shane were already on a countdown.

Her hand faltered over the phone. It would be the considerate thing to let him know she was going to be late back, right? Then why did it feel as if she was suddenly treating him like someone she was in a long-term committed relationship with? By ringing him to 'report in' would she be overstepping where they currently were? Would she be giving him the impression that she was more involved than she could let herself be?

Where were they, after all, beyond being in a very sexually charged place where none of the real problems had been resolved?

Why was she over-thinking a simple courtesy call?

With a shake of her head she picked up the phone and punched in the numbers. Reasoning with herself that it was only good manners. Though she did feel marginally better when she got the answer machine.

By half past eight the shipment still hadn't arrived. Everyone had their work cleared away and some of the next morning's work done and a lethargy had fallen over the large store rooms. And Shane hadn't called her back.

Surely it would have been equally polite of him to have called her back? Damn him.

Maybe it would be easier if he behaved like a typical thoughtless man so she would find it easier to walk away.

She was alone in the room where goods were checked in when his voice sounded behind her. 'Well, you look busy.'

The sound made her jump in her seat. Spinning around on her stool, she stared at him with wide eyes, her heart beating harder at the sight of him. 'What are you doing here? We're not supposed to have friends come visit.'

His wide shoulders shrugged. 'You have to eat.'

Her gaze fell to a bag that he lifted in front of his body and a checked rug that was thrown over his arm, 'You brought me food?'

'Have you eaten?'

'No.' Her stomach growled in response.

'Damn, guess I *should* have brought some food then.'

A quick glance at the sparkle in his eyes was enough for her to know he was kidding. And her heart warmed; it was quite possibly one of the nicest things anyone had ever done for her. She raised her chin and blinked slowly. 'So, what did you bring me? Anything nice?'

With a small smile he walked across to her, leaned his face so close that his nose almost touched hers. Then tilted his head, his gaze focusing on her parted lips. 'Unfortunately only stuff that's decent under all your security cameras.'

'Damn again, then.'

He finally smiled. 'You're right there.'

Finn tilted her head in the opposite direction to his, her eyes narrowing slightly as a thought occurred to her. 'How did you get in here?'

'I told them I was your boyfriend.'

'Did you, now?'

'Yep.'

'And they said?'

'One of them said you were a lucky girl.'

Finn giggled. Something she hadn't done in a good fifteen years.

Shane smiled in response, his dimples creasing, 'I agreed with her.'

Quirking her eyebrows, she looked down, conscious of

the fact he kept looking at her face as she did. 'So what's in the bag?'

'Uh-uh.' He waited until her chin rose again, pointing a long finger at his good cheek. 'Kiss first.'

With a slow smile and a glimpse to the flickering light on the camera in the corner, she leaned in the last couple of inches and pressed her mouth to his. His mouth was still for a moment, his body tensing, then he relaxed and moved his lips with hers in a soft, brief touch that left her wanting a lot more.

When he lifted his head back he whispered in a low grumble, 'What about the cameras?'

'You told them you're my boyfriend. They won't expect anything less.'

He smiled softly, lifted his finger again to brush it over her sensitive lips. 'Now I wish I'd told them I was your gynaecologist.'

Laughter filled the air as he stepped back and spread the checked rug on the floor behind them. Then he dug in his bag and produced packet sandwiches, crisps, a bar of her favourite chocolate, two cans of soda and a tea-light candle.

Which he lit, then raised an eyebrow as he looked up at her. 'Ta-da. Picnic à la Dwyer.'

Watching him from her stool, Finn wondered at the mystery that was Shane Dwyer. She'd thought she knew him before but apparently she'd only got half the story.

'So you do this kind of thing for all your girlfriends?'

'No, I already took take-away to the other two.'

'It's amazing you don't weigh about three hundred pounds.'

He waited until they were both sitting on the rug, Finn

hiding her eyes from him as she reached for a packet of sandwiches. 'What?'

The sandwiches refused to be opened, so Finn focused all her attention on them and avoided looking at Shane. His words had been meant as a joke, she knew that. But they had stolen away some of the glow she'd felt at him referring to himself as her boyfriend. Maybe that had just been a joke to him too.

She knew he had dated before, plenty. Though the thought of him with someone else had never affected her before. Much. Well, much that she'd admitted to herself. But it bothered her more and more on an almost daily basis now.

'I can't get these open.'

His hand reached over and took the packet from her, ripping it open in one fluid motion before he handed them back. 'What?'

'Nothing—stupid sandwiches.' She scowled down at the guilty sandwich packet that had been so easy for *him* to open. Then flashed him a quick smile before biting into one, momentarily escaping having to make any further explanation.

Shane's eyes narrowed. 'Not the kind of sandwiches you like?'

She swallowed. 'They're grand.'

He wasn't buying the smile she gave him. 'Talk to me. I can't read your mind.'

Suddenly she felt like an immature idiot. In every other 'relationship' she'd ever had she'd known exactly where she stood, had felt she had some semblance of control. But just because she was reacting inside like some nervous teenager with her first ever boyfriend didn't mean she should act like it on the outside.

'I'm just being stupid; don't worry about it.'

His mouth quirked. 'I never have before.'

'Ha, ha.'

'So what is it?'

'Apart from the fact that this is really new territory, you mean?'

'No one else ever fed you in work before?'

'No, I can honestly say that this is a first.'

'You've been seeing the wrong guys, I told you that already.'

'No, you said I was seeing them to avoid facing up to the fact I fancied you.' She shrugged. 'Or something along those lines.'

Ripping open his own sandwiches, he studied her for a long moment, then dived on in with a big one. 'And was I right?'

The question stopped her in her tracks. That would be a big confession, now wouldn't it?

'Maybe.'

Shane let the softly spoken word hang in the air for a while, his heart beating hard and loud. He knew the maybe was a yes, could see it in her eyes. And he wanted to haul her forward and kiss her senseless for it. It was good to know he wasn't alone. She might not have been as obsessed as he'd once tried telling himself he hadn't been. But she had been attracted and that was a big thing. Huge. It gave what was happening with them a more equal basis.

It made it potentially *serious*.

A word he had managed to avoid for most of his life.

'Even though you were so determined not to fancy a firefighter?'

'I'm still not past that part, so maybe it would be better not to talk about it right this minute.'

All right, he was happy enough with that. There was still plenty of time to persuade her that the world wasn't going to fall on his head any time soon.

His pause left an opening for her. 'How come I feel like I really don't know you all that well?'

'You know me.'

'Not that well, I don't.'

'You know me a hell of a lot better than you did twenty-four hours ago.'

Her cheeks flushed a soft pink. He loved it when she did that. There weren't too many women around who blushed any more. In fact it was only recently that he'd even managed to get Finn to blush. He loved that he had even that simple a physical effect on her.

'That goes both ways.'

Leaning towards her, he lowered his voice to the same intimate drawl he'd used on the phone. 'Tell me that camera isn't on and we can learn some more.'

Her eyes sparkled, then blinked a couple of times as she cleared her head, leaving him wondering what she'd been thinking. 'You're avoiding talking.'

'Well, we could talk about it if the camera had no sound.'

'So long as what we're talking about is sex.'

'It's one of my favourite topics of discussion with you.'

There was a small snort of laughter. 'Recently it's been pretty much the only topic of conversation with me. Try talking about something else.'

He leaned back. 'Like what?'

'Anything—you can even choose.' She leaned towards him, her eyes wide for a moment. 'I really don't know much beyond what I can see on the outside. How come I never realized that before now?'

'I could say the same thing about you.'

'No, you couldn't. You know everything there is to know about me. You know my family; you know what I do for a living—' she flung a hand out to one side '—you even know what most of my underwear looks like now!'

He couldn't help himself. 'Not while you're wearing it I don't.'

Long lashes blinked at him for a long, long time. And without her even speaking he knew he'd said the wrong thing. She really wanted to know more about him and his making with the funnies wasn't getting him out of it. 'What do you want to know?'

Her gaze softened. 'We could start with why it is I know so little?'

A shrug. 'I guess I'm not much of a talker.'

'Eddie probably knows more than me.'

'That's different.'

'Different, how?'

'We work together, we used to live in the same house—' he was almost tempted to tell her it was because Eddie was a guy, but that wouldn't really be true '—but I don't know that he knows me that much better than you do. I'm not much of a talker.'

'You already said that.'

'Well, there you go, then.' He held his hands up in surrender. 'I rest my case.'

There was a moment while thoughts crossed her expressive eyes. Then a sparkle began in their green depths and a smile teased the corners of her lips, catching his attention.

She leaned towards him, her lush breasts tilting teasingly into his line of vision. He stared at the 'V' of her plain white blouse, was tempted to raise his chin a little to see if he could catch a glimpse of lace. But her lilting voice brought his attention back to her face.

'We'll just have to see if I can find a way to *persuade* you to share information.'

'Like what, for instance?'

'I'm thinking of a reward system…'

Reward system? Damn, he'd almost tell her anything if there were rewards of the kind he wanted involved.

In fact a list was already forming…

Finn smiled as if she knew about the list and what was on it. Her eyes sparkled with enthusiasm, her lips parted to show her even teeth. And Shane had a sudden, swift desire to keep that look on her face as long as possible. Even if it did mean breaking the habit of a lifetime and sharing personal information.

She was worth the effort.

CHAPTER ELEVEN

'I'M DEFINITELY due some of those rewards.'

'You think?' Finn laughed as Shane grabbed hold of her inside the door, spinning her around until she had her back against the solid oak. 'I've already thanked you for staying to help out.'

Raising his hands to place them, palms flat, against the door either side of her head, he then leaned the length of his body against her so that she was pinned in place.

'It was fun.'

'I think it was more fun for the girls you flirted with than it was for you.'

'It wasn't them I stayed to be with.'

Smiling up at him, she smoothed her palms down his ribcage, the taut muscles of his abdomen flexing. 'That gets a reward all right.'

Her fingers undid a button on his shirt.

Shane tilted his chin down to look at her hands as her fingers slid to another button. With his chin still down he glanced up at her from between thick dark lashes. 'A button? That's my reward for counting hundreds of CDs?'

'What was the name of the first girl you kissed?'

He smiled a slow smile as the memory entered his mind. 'Mary McCauley.'

Another button was freed. 'What age were you?'

'Six.'

'No, you weren't!' She gave him a look of outrage. 'No one has their first proper kiss at six.'

'Maybe I just started early?'

'Not that early, you didn't.'

'Okay—' he rocked his head from side to side '—she was my second cousin and after one family get-together all the grown-ups thought it would be cute if we kissed for the camera.'

Finn smiled.

'I had to stand on a telephone book to reach her and I wiped my mouth with the back of my hand after. It was very romantic.'

She laughed and slipped another button free, her fingers grazing against his warm skin. She looked down to check her progress, her voice thickening. 'First proper kiss?'

'Sinead Begley, in fourth year at high school. She was the year above me and I even tried a quick grope. Again, very romantic.'

Another button, and she smoothed the edges of the shirt back from his ribs, her eyes moving over the ridges of his abs and down to where a hint of dark hair dipped into the belt of his jeans. 'First serious relationship.'

'Define serious.'

Her eyes flickered upwards. 'Girlfriend. Someone you saw for a few months. Someone you really liked.'

His lashes blinked lazily. 'I've never dated for longer than a few months.'

'How come?'

It took a long time for him to answer. 'Just wasn't right, I s'pose.'

Unreasonably, part of her ached to have him say it was because he'd never met someone like her before. She slipped another button free. 'First time you made love?'

'Uh-uh. Not telling you that.' He started on some of her buttons, his fingers working faster than hers. 'That one can be a minefield.'

Okay, he had a point there. So she jumped into something that she had been thinking about after all his explicit phone calls. 'First time you thought about making love with me?'

His hands smoothed her blouse and jacket open while he fixed her with a sensual gaze. 'That's easy. At the shorts and shades party we threw for Eddie's thirtieth.'

Finn's eye's widened. Hang on, that had been over a year ago!

Shane smiled while his hands cupped her breasts, caressing her through yet another lacy concoction of his own choosing. 'We were playing truths…'

It was yet another of Eddie's dumb games. It consisted of someone making a statement like, 'I've never had sex on a first date' and everyone who had had to take a drink. A game that became all the more bawdy when it was played in a large group of people who knew each other pretty damn well so that when someone didn't drink and someone else knew better a challenge ensued. And secrets were told. And the person who lied had to down a glassful.

It was why Finn had never not taken a drink when it was something she'd done. She wasn't that great a drinker to end up downing glass after glass.

His fingers found her nipples and teased them into

aching peaks. 'You drank to "I've never faked an orgasm" and I told myself that would never happen when you were with me.'

Finn's fingers faltered. The irony was she remembered it too. Every woman there had silently taken a drink, not just her. Then they'd all laughed for a good ten minutes.

And she remembered looking across at Shane, thinking she'd bet no girl of his ever had to take a drink for that one.

So just how long had *she* been thinking about it?

His dimples quirked. 'After that I couldn't stop looking at you. I had all sorts of interesting fantasies.'

'You're kidding.'

'Nope.' He moved a hand round to unclasp her bra, opening it with a flick of his fingers and a wink. 'You were forbidden territory and that was erotic as hell.'

'Forbidden why?' She abandoned the shirt buttons and headed south, her fingers slipping under the edge of his jeans to slide back and forth.

With a sharp intake of breath he turned them round and backed to the stairs, his mouth descending to her neck where he mumbled, 'You're my best friend's sister. I'm going to get my ass kicked for this at some stage.'

It was an aspect she hadn't thought of in a while, wrapped up as she was in eroticism and her own warring emotions. Eddie was going to go mad when he found out. Hell, what was she thinking? They weren't going to last long enough for a problem that big to be an issue. 'What he doesn't know won't hurt him.'

Her hands were on his belt buckle as he lowered her to the stairs. When his tongue drew a line from her ear to her collar-bone her breath caught, heat pooling where she wanted him. No matter what wrongs there were in their relationship, this part was just so right. Talking on the phone had had her ready for him all day long.

Raising his head for a second, he smiled seductively at her. 'About this orgasm thing.'

Finn swallowed hard. 'Uh-huh?'

He branded her lips with a searing kiss. 'Never, ever with me. You hear?'

When his head descended to lave her breast, she let her head drop back onto the stair and gasped in answer, 'I don't see that being a problem.'

By the time he had unbuttoned her trousers, pushed them in one confident sweep to her calves along with her panties and pushed her legs open to set his mouth to her she knew that the only orgasm problem she would ever have with Shane would possibly be dying from one.

But as she finished crying out his name and he kissed his way up her body to her mouth, his whispered words froze the blood in her heated veins. 'Now, as to the Eddie issue, I'll talk to him and sort it out.'

Her eyes flew open. 'No, you won't.'

His head rose an inch. 'I'm not having him figure this out on his own; that would be worse.'

Yes, it would. As far as Finn was concerned, Eddie not finding out and still not knowing was absolutely the best scenario. Shane wouldn't be the only one getting an ass-kicking otherwise.

But while her body still hummed and his eyes were looking into hers with unspoken questions she found she couldn't say something as honest as, 'What's the point when this won't last?'

'Wait a while.'

He continued to look at her while her fingers

smoothed his thick hair back. 'You want us to just keep sneaking around?'

Finn smiled. 'There's a certain amount of fun in that, don't you think?'

'Yes—' the word came out on an almost reluctant note '—but I don't think you want to hurt someone we both care about any more than I do.'

'I don't.'

'But you still want to wait?'

'Yes.'

'Why?'

She should have known he'd ask. There were a great many things she didn't know about him, things she was loving learning, but there were just as many things she did know. And one of those things was that he not only cared for her brother, he respected him. He was an honourable man when it came to Eddie and his service mates. They all were.

She tried to smooth it over with, 'I just think it's too early.'

While she sent up a silent plea that he wouldn't push it any further, an *unlikely* miracle, he continued studying her face.

Finn could feel herself squirming inwardly. The fact that she was lying, mostly unclothed, on the stairs while he still had pretty much all of his on only added to her vulnerability.

As if he could read the thoughts in her eyes, he slowly began to put her clothing back in place, his eyes dropping to consider his progress.

He took a breath. 'You still don't get this, do you?'

Her green eyes blinked at his dark hair while she said nothing in reply.

'Yeah, that's what I thought.' Gathering the edges of her

blouse together, he stood up and headed up the rest of the stairs alone.

For a few heartbeats Finn stayed where she was, stunned. She had absolutely no idea what had just happened. One minute they'd been headed for another night of endless mutual pleasure and now…

What did he mean she didn't 'get it'?

'What did you mean by that?' She stood in the open doorway of his room, still doing up the buttons on her blouse with shaky fingers.

Shane shrugged, throwing his bunched up shirt onto the end of his bed. 'You don't, that's all.'

'All I said was I thought it was too early to tell Eddie. And it is.'

'That's not what you meant, though.'

Finn was getting more frustrated by the minute. 'I have no idea what you mean and how can I if you don't say what's on your mind? Just spit it out.'

'Okay, then.' He stepped towards her with determined strides, his eyes glinting dangerously. 'It's got nothing to do with it being too early or that it's "fun" sneaking around. You don't want him to know because you think this is something that will only last until *you* say it's done.'

Finn gaped at his intuition.

His laughter was harsh. 'Yeah, that's what I figured. What I don't have figured out is how long you're going to cling to this not-being-involved-with-me-'cos-I'm-a-fire-fighter excuse.'

'Excuse?' Her voice finally reappeared and with it her anger. 'You think I'm using it as an *excuse*?'

One dark eyebrow quirked at her in challenge.

'*Fine*.' She turned around, ready to march down the hall

and as far away from him as possible. Until his words stopped her.

'Now there's a word I haven't heard you use in a while. Your favourite word to use when you don't want to talk.'

Stopping dead, she swung on him. 'As opposed to your method of not talking at all!'

'I've done nothing but bloody talk all night!' Leaning his face closer, he added, 'Not that you've paid that much attention to anything else that's been goin' on.'

Oh, she'd been paying attention. She'd listened to every word he'd said, had watched every glance, memorized every touch. As if she was making up a mental album of memories that she could delve into when it was all done. What amongst all of it had she missed? Shane seemed certain she'd missed something.

And, dared she believe it, was *hurt* that she had?

'Well, why don't you try telling me now?'

His head shook again. 'You're so smart, you figure it out. You've been so good at thinking everything through without my help so far. You told me you wouldn't get involved until I quit the service. Then you said it was because if I got hurt you wouldn't be able to take it. Then when I did get a bit of a battering you threw yourself straight at me—'

'*Threw* myself at you!' It was true, but knowing that didn't make it sting any less. '*You* didn't help any?'

'You knew where I stood, Finn. It wasn't like you didn't have any warning. But you told yourself it was fine because it wouldn't last long, didn't you?'

'Because I should have expected more from the king of lasting relationships?'

The words, spat at him with such venom, seemed to halt him in his tracks. He shook his head again, ran a frustrated hand back through his hair, spiking it ridiculously while his eyes avoided hers.

Then, while the moment of silence allowed them both to take some calming breaths, he looked back into her eyes. His voice was flat. 'So this is what to you, then—some kind of itch to scratch?'

The fact that he was using the phraseology she herself had used to Mel as something *he* would do didn't pass her by unnoticed. Blinking slowly at him, she knew he was giving her the perfect opportunity to end it. Which was what she already knew she had to do, right?

So, how come she couldn't seem to bring herself to take the opportunity?

Sensing tears building at the back of her eyes, she continued blinking to hold them back. 'You want me to build my life around someone like you, to rely on you being there for ever?'

It was Shane's turn to stay silent.

'You see that's just the thing, isn't it? You can't make me a guarantee to be around for ever, even if it was in you to do that.'

He still didn't speak.

Finn swallowed hard. 'Even if you could, Shane, there would always be a part of me I'd have to hold back. Because I *know*—' despite her best efforts, her voice cracked and she had to pause to clear her throat '—I know what it's like to lose someone who's the centre of your universe. And it hurts. It hurts way more than I ever want to hurt again. So this is it for me.'

His eyes moved to where her hand moved back and forth between them. Then back to her face again as she raised her other hand to wipe at one eye.

'Whatever this is, it's all I can give.' She pursed her lips and finished with, 'So, you can take it or leave it. It's up to you.'

When he still didn't speak, her chin dropped and she stepped back. Only to have his arm shoot out, his hand grasping hers.

Her gaze rose, looking back and forth at his eyes with unspoken questions.

He tugged, brought her back into the room, using his free hand to close the door behind her. And still said nothing.

So with a breathy sigh she leaned forwards and communicated with him the only way she could.

CHAPTER TWELVE

Two weeks in and Shane was still asking himself why it was he found it so difficult to tell Finn how he felt. He'd known when she'd talked about building her life around someone like him, relying on him being there for ever.

He was in love with her.

Lying in the dim light of a rapidly rising dawn, watching her sleeping beside him, he knew the emotion was only getting bigger every day.

Watching her sleep was one of his favourite things to do. Sometimes he thought his body woke up so early specifically so he could watch her. So he could memorize how she looked while she slept.

The toughest thing about watching her was stopping himself from touching her. With Finn it wasn't a case of familiarity breeding boredom; he wanted her more each time he made love with her. And she didn't seem to complain.

Her breasts rose as she took a deeper breath in her sleep and she rolled towards him, settling her head deeper into the pillow.

She was beautiful.

Even with her face devoid of make-up and her hair tumbling in untamed lengths over her shoulder and the pillow.

The first night he had watched her sleep he had been fascinated by the expressions she would make; when she would crinkle her nose or a smile would lift the edges of her mouth. Almost as if in slumber she was experiencing things he couldn't see.

The thought that some of those dreams might have him in them made the not touching her even more difficult.

But she was looking tired of late, her workload and the hours they spent making love beginning to catch up on her. So he had to make do with smiling when she smiled. Allowing himself to brush her hair back from her cheek while he wondered what it would take to get her to change her mind about what she could give him.

Because he wanted it all. For the first time in his life he wanted someone to share everything with.

They had everything going for them. Apart from the most amazing physical compatibility, they had a shared sense of humour, an ability to spend time in each other's company without having to make small talk, shared interests in things like films and books. Even the fact that there were differences in their personalities only seemed to add to the package.

It was just the lack of any honest communication that held them apart.

And Shane had no idea how to get past that, communication on something so close to the heart hardly being something he had much experience in.

When her eyes opened a couple of hours later she found him looking down at her with a soft smile on his face. She groaned and closed her eyes again. 'Please tell me I wasn't drooling.'

He laughed. 'I might be flattered if you were.'

Turning her face into the pillow, she chuckled. It was the third time she'd woken up to find him looking at her and each time she'd made a joke about what she feared she'd been doing while he watched.

And at least while they were laughing she wasn't thinking about how it felt to wake up and look straight into his eyes.

Because every morning she did it hurt a little more. And every day she had to smile her way through it, telling herself it didn't mean anything when he smiled at her the way he did. He was just a great guy. She'd always known that. She just hadn't ever thought about how it would feel to be in a relationship with him that was purely based on sex. With emotions constantly buried for survival.

She peeked out from the pillow, her voice muffled. 'How long have you been awake?'

'A while. Not long.' He smiled through the lie.

Her face gradually reappeared. She smoothed her cheek against the pillow and blinked slowly, smiling back. 'What time does your shift start?'

'I'm filling in for Callum from one. You're on a late start today, right?'

Finn nodded. 'Just before lunchtime.'

His eyes sparkled down at her and she chuckled. So he leaned down and kissed her softly, gently nipping her bottom lip before he lifted his head again. 'How about I bring us some breakfast in bed and then we can take a shower together before you go to work?'

The suggestion woke her body up fully. Would she ever get tired of making love with him? It was a question that had been worrying her of late. Surely the thrill should have been wearing off by now?

'I'll make breakfast. It's my turn.'

'I knew I liked you for a reason.'

Grinning, she stole another quick kiss before she swung her legs off the bed and grabbed his shirt, buttoning it up as she walked barefoot into the hall.

She was still smiling as she closed the door behind her and turned.

To look straight into her brother's stunned face.

The colour drained from her face. '*Eddie*—'

He stared at her for what felt like a lifetime. Then he pointed aimlessly down the hall. 'I came to get a couple of boxes I left behind. I figured everyone was still asleep so…'

Finn swallowed hard as his words faded. 'Eddie—'

He held his palm up, shook his head. 'Don't, Finn. I don't want to hear it.'

'Eddie, wait!' She called his name softly as he turned on his heel and jogged swiftly back down the stairs.

There was really nothing else she could do but follow him, her voice rising more confidently when she was away from Shane's door. 'Damn it, Eddie, wait a minute!'

She was halfway down the stairs, could see his hand on the handle of the front door. Then he turned, glared up at her and marched into the middle of the living room.

Finn followed him, stopping when the sofa was between them. 'I didn't want you to find out like this.'

'Find out what exactly?' He crossed his arms across his chest and continued glaring. 'No, on second thought, don't bother 'cos I already get it.'

She couldn't think what to say.

Eddie's voice rose. 'Are you bloody out of your mind?'

It was certainly a pertinent question. 'Eddie—'

'I mean, how stupid are you? You know Shane! You

know what he's like with women and he's a bloody firefighter, for God's sake! You said you would never get involved with one and I said that was good 'cos I'd never let you get involved with one after you explained why!'

'I remember. But this isn't what you think it is.'

Her retort raised the colour in his cheeks. 'Oh, really?'

'Yes, really.' She crossed her arms in a similar way to his and cocked a hip. 'I know what I'm doing.'

She amazed herself by not flinching at the lie.

Eddie's eyes strayed to the stairs behind her, rage flaring as he pointed upwards. 'You better stay the hell away from here while I talk to my sister. I'll deal with you later, *pal*.'

Head snapping round, she found Shane behind her. He'd managed jeans and a T-shirt, which made him less guiltily clothed than her. But the damage was already done.

His blue eyes flickered briefly to hers, then met Eddie's with a steady gaze. 'Leave her be, Eddie. You want to yell at someone, then yell at me.'

Finn managed to keep her voice calm. 'I'm fine, Shane.'

'You're not doing this alone.' He walked slowly down the last few steps.

Eddie laughed cruelly. 'Well, aren't you two just the sweetest thing?'

'I was going to talk to you abou—' Shane started.

But Finn finished, 'But I wouldn't let him.'

'Sneaking around behind my back was much better.'

'We weren't sneaking around to hurt you on purpose.' She focused her attention on Eddie as Shane reached her side. 'Eddie, this isn't some great plot. It just happened, that's all. It's no big deal.'

'Really?' They both spoke in unison.

And Finn didn't know which one of them to look at.

'I think you and me need a bit of a talk before we speak to Eddie.'

The statement made her mind up for her, her face turning towards Shane. 'No, we don't. You know what's happening here; we already talked about it.'

'That was a while ago.'

Eddie gaped. '"A while ago?" How bloody long has this been going on?'

'Nothing's changed.' She looked Shane in the eyes momentarily, then glanced at her brother. 'And not all that long.'

'It was going on when me and Kathy had the party, wasn't it? I thought I saw something then, but I told myself I was being stupid. 'Cos my sister knew better and my best friend wouldn't dare!'

She really couldn't deal with both of them at once. 'Eddie, calm yourself. I'm not a little kid and I can do whatever I want.'

She took a step back from Shane and frowned at him. 'And you needn't bother going over this with me again. We both know exactly where we stand.'

'Do we?'

The question astounded her, her voice rising in slight panic and a tint of anger. 'Yes, we do! This was never going to last long.'

'Oh, well, that's great. Now it's just a quick shag. I feel much better now.'

'Shut up, Eddie.' This time Shane and Finn spoke in unison, not even looking Eddie's way.

Eddie's arms uncrossed and he stepped round the sofa. Immediately Shane stepped between him and Finn, his shoulders rising as he held a hand to Eddie's chest. In a flash Eddie had the hand thrown off and pushed Shane back.

Finn stepped into the fray, a hand on each of their chests. 'Would you two quit it? This is ridiculous. You're friends, for crying out loud.'

'Not any more, we're not.' Eddie stepped back as he threw the words over her shoulder.

Shane sighed. 'We'll talk about this one alone, Eddie. I know you're spitting. I knew you would be.'

'Yeah, and you know why too. You broke the rules on this, Shane; you're way outta line.'

'I know that.'

'Then why did you do it?'

Finn shook her head. 'He didn't do it alone.'

'I've seen him in action before, don't you forget. I used to live here.'

'And he's hardly the first person I've ever slept with either.'

Eddie looked as if any second he might explode and leave 'goo' on the walls. 'Why *him*, Finn? Why couldn't you just keep on dating those librarian blokes?'

'Right now I wish I had.' She sighed.

'You don't mean that and you know you don't.'

Shane had a small half-smile on his face when she looked at him.

'Don't do that.' With a small sigh she looked back at her brother. 'This has happened and that's that. I can't change it.'

'Would you change it if you could?'

It was a fair enough question. One that she might even have answered in the affirmative up until recently. But not now. Not now she had so many memories of being with him, of what it felt like being with him.

'If it hadn't happened I think I would have spent a long

time wondering what it would have been like. And that wouldn't have been healthy. This way it won't screw up any future relationships I have with other librarians.'

She felt Shane tense beneath the hand she still held on his chest. So she let it drop, glancing at his face from the corner of her eye.

He, in turn, stared at her with a stony expression. 'You're planning on there being other librarians, are you?' Tilting his head, he added a sarcastic, 'So soon, my love?'

Her heart twisted painfully. 'Stop it.'

But he continued with a quirk of his eyebrows. 'Anyone in particular in mind?'

'Anyone would be preferable to her staying with you. All you'll end up doing is leaving her high and dry. It's what you know best, after all. Like father, like son, right?'

Finn's eyes widened in shock as Shane's jaw clenched, his hands bunching into fists at his sides as he glared venomously at Eddie. 'Don't go there.'

Eddie ignored the warning, hitting hurt with hurt. 'Or maybe you thought if you slept with Finn you'd be sleeping your way into a happy family?'

Shane swore viciously, took a step forward, 'I get that you're mad with me, Eddie. But you have no idea what happened with Finn and me. And it has nothing to do with my past, so leave it the hell alone.'

Eddie seemed to realize he'd overstepped the mark. His tone changed, anger giving way to coolness. 'I don't want to know what happened, Shane. The damage is done.'

'I know.' His jaw clenched again, his eyes flickering to Finn. 'In more ways than one.'

Finn watched him turn away. Watched him walk back upstairs without so much as a backwards glance. And the urge to follow him was so strong she even felt her body sway forwards.

But Eddie's firm hand on her arm stopped her. 'Leave him be, Finn.'

She turned her head to look at him, recognizing regret on his face. 'What have you just done?'

'Said something I shouldn't.'

'Oh, I got that bit.'

Eddie's gaze became more determined. 'You should never have let this happen.'

With a shaky breath she confessed the truth. 'I couldn't stop it.'

'Bloody hell, Finn.' The words came out on a sigh. 'He's the best mate I ever had.'

'It doesn't have anything to do with you and him.'

'Yes, it does. You just don't get it, do you? He broke one of the biggest rules. All the guys know it. Everyone *knows* not to break it. You don't sleep around with a sister of a mate and you don't sleep around with a mate's ex. It makes for bad feeling and that messes things up in work.'

When she frowned at his reasoning he added, 'And the brigade is all the family Shane has. It means more to him than anything else ever could.'

Finn blinked at him with wide eyes. She'd known the service was a family for all of them, but—

'And how could *you* do it, Finn? You, the one who still makes me call you after every shift? The one who, of all of us, has never got over what happened to Dad? What are you, some kind of *masochist*?' He shook his head. 'I just don't get this at all.'

Neither did Finn. That was just the problem.

CHAPTER THIRTEEN

FINN was on the end of his bed when Shane came out of the shower. She was still dressed in his shirt.

The hand that had been rubbing a towel through his hair stilled and he stared at her pale face. 'Eddie didn't throw you over his shoulder and take you off somewhere safe, then?'

'I wouldn't let him.'

He swallowed. 'Maybe you should have.'

'He's sorry about what he said, you know.'

Shane shrugged and continued rubbing his hair vigorously as he walked to his wardrobe. 'People say things when they're angry. I'll survive.'

'Why didn't you ever tell me about your father?'

'It never came up in a game of truths.' He threw the towel on the ground and yanked open the wardrobe door.

'When did he leave?'

'It doesn't matter when he left; he just did.'

'Eddie says that's the reason the brigade is so important to you.'

'Eddie needs to stop watching Oprah.'

'Is it why you've never had a serious relationship?'

'What difference does it make to you? You're the one doing the walking this time, not me.'

Finn watched as he yanked a brigade shirt from the wardrobe and draped it over his shoulders. Even before she'd heard her brother throw the new information into the argument downstairs she'd known that they had hit the end of the road. The very fact that Eddie had reacted the way he had, with both of them, and the fact that he had then pointed out all the truths to her, had pretty much been the clincher.

It had always been her who was going to walk away. She had known that from the start, even while she'd known that if she'd taken a chance and stayed Shane would eventually have been the one to walk.

By walking first, Finn had told herself she still had control over *something*. So why was it so hard to take the steps when a path opened up?

Shane glanced over his shoulder. 'If you need a few more days here I can stay at the station.'

'Kathy bought a sofa bed, apparently.'

He looked away. 'That's handy. Shame she didn't buy it a bit earlier.'

The flippant statement hurt. He didn't mean it, but he had to know it would hurt. 'Yeah, well, hindsight is a great thing.'

'Your house insurance should be through soon anyway.' Keeping his back to her, he moved to a drawer and pulled out a pair of familiar white boxers, hauling them up under his towel. Discarding the towel, he then moved back to the wardrobe. 'Eddie and Kathy won't mind you there 'til you find a new place.'

'I'm going to Mum's for Christmas soon.'

'Send her my love.'

Finn swallowed hard, nodded at his back. 'I will.'

'Tell her I'm sorry I won't be making it down there for Christmas dinner this year.'

It was a massive thing. Ever since he'd met Eddie at the brigade training centre he'd been dragged along for Christmas dinner. He only ever stayed the one day but Finn's mum loved it when he was there, heaping his plate with food and showering him with socks and ridiculous winter sweaters just as she did with her other three 'boys'.

For him not to be there would be like missing a member of the family. It wouldn't just be Finn that would feel his absence.

'Shane—' Her voice shook on his name.

'It's probably not a good idea to have me and Eddie slugging it out across the dinner table. This'll just take a wee while to blow over, is all.' He pulled on dark trousers and turned to face her as he zipped them up, tucking his shirt in. 'Maybe next year, eh?'

She didn't know what she expected to see on his face when he turned around. Or what she hoped to see. But she didn't expect him to be so very calm.

He blinked slowly at her, his eyes giving nothing away, not a hint of emotion, before he walked back to his dresser and lifted a comb. Looking briefly at her reflection in the mirror, he stroked his spiking hair into place.

'I'm gonna head into work early. Maybe see if I can catch Eddie for a talk later before he sets the rest of the hounds on me.'

'He told me about the rule.'

'Mmm.' He nodded.

'And even when what those guys think matters to you so much you still took a chance?'

He smiled a small smile at her reflection. 'Well, you can try explainin' it to a little kid, but they don't really get that fire burns 'til they stick their hand in it. Do they?'

She suddenly had a hundred questions she wanted to ask him. A hundred things her heart wanted her to know.

But he set the comb back in place and turned to look at her face again. 'This will all blow over; don't worry about it. It just needs a bit of time. Really.'

Out of the hundred the one that jumped straight to the front of her mind was, 'Do you want me to stay?' If he'd asked her to she doubted she'd have been able to leave. Not this way anyway.

'Shane—'

'I better go. And you'll be late for work if you don't get a move on.' He smiled another small smile and turned to leave the room.

Then he stopped in the hallway, his back to her as he spoke in a husky voice. 'All the best with the next librarian, babe.'

Finn stayed on the end of his bed, still wearing the shirt that surrounded her in his scent. She sat there for a long time as the silence of the house surrounded her.

Then she dropped her head into her hands and cried until she had no more tears to shed.

The one thing she'd had right was how much it would hurt when she lost him. Not that there was much comfort in knowing she'd been right about the one thing.

The whole thing sucked. Big time.

'We'll get the spare room cleared out for you as soon as we can.' Kathy smiled as she set out bedclothes for the sofa bed. 'If I'd known you were coming I'd have got Eddie to do it sooner.'

'Don't worry about it. It's not like anyone could have seen this one coming.'

Kathy hesitated. Then she sat down on the edge of the

sofa beside Finn. She seemed to wrestle with the idea of saying something and Finn felt for her. They really didn't know each other well enough to have a deep conversation.

'It's okay; you don't have to give me a shoulder to cry on. I'm fine.'

Kathy studied her face. 'Are you sure? You don't look fine to me.'

Actually she couldn't remember the last time she'd really been *fine*. She'd used the word plenty of late, but had never meant it when she'd said it.

Swallowing a thick lump in her throat, she looked down at her hands, twining her fingers in and out of each other. 'I'm just having a rough couple of months, I guess.' She smiled a weak smile. 'They say bad things come in threes don't they? I s'pose that means I've still got one to go. That's something to look forward to, right?'

'Old wives' tale. Don't you believe it.'

'You just wait and see. I'm on a roll…'

Kathy smiled. 'Look, don't worry about Eddie. He'll calm down after a bit. I think he's just annoyed he didn't see it coming. He would never have let Shane hurt you like this.'

Finn's eyes widened at the statement, her head turning to look at Kathy's face. 'You think Shane hurt me?' She blinked in surprise as Kathy nodded. 'Kathy, Shane didn't make this mess. *I* did.'

'I don't understand. Eddie says that Shane never stays with anyone, he's the love-'em-and-leave-'em type, 'cos of the way his dad was when he was growing up.'

Oh, come on! Was she the *only* one that didn't know about Shane's past? Even Kathy, who had barely known him five minutes, seemed to know more than she did. Thanks to Eddie, no doubt.

Eddie, who could have mentioned it to his *own sister* at some point.

Finn shook her head. 'It was me that ended it. Or, more to the point, it was me that wouldn't let it be serious in the first place. I swore I wouldn't get that deeply involved with him and he knew that.'

'Well, maybe it suited him that way. No strings.'

Finn shook her head again, a frown of concentration on her face. 'I don't think so. He kept arguing with me about it, saying that I was using excuses.'

'And what *was* your excuse?'

'It wasn't an excuse!'

'I'm sorry.' Kathy looked even more uncomfortable than she had when she'd sat down. 'I didn't mean to suggest—'

'No, don't. I'm sorry.' She reached a hand across and squeezed one of Kathy's. 'I shouldn't have snapped at you; it's not your fault.'

Another hand rose to enclose Finn's as Kathy leaned her head in closer. 'Don't worry about it.'

'I'm just a bit messed up right now.' She flashed another small smile. 'Though if you didn't tell Eddie that it would be helpful.'

'You tell me not to tell him and I won't. Promise.'

'Thanks.' For the twentieth time since she'd first met her, Finn was struck by how lucky her brother had got with Kathy. She really was very lovely. And thoughtful. And she'd not only fallen for her dopey brother, she'd fallen for her dopey brother *the firefighter*.

Finn suddenly wondered how she felt about that part. Did he have to make two phone calls after every shift now? Or was his coming home enough for Kathy?

But then maybe Kathy just didn't know any better?

Finn didn't ask.

Having already messed up two relationships in one day she wasn't keen to try for a third. 'I appreciate it.'

'No problem.' And with a final squeeze of Finn's hand she stood up and walked away. 'There are more blankets in the hot press if you get cold. Those big windows to the balcony can let a bit of a chill in on cold nights.'

'Thanks, Kathy. 'Night.'

''Night.'

For a while she pondered over the question of extra blankets. Cold December nights hadn't been an issue for a couple of weeks. Because she'd had Shane's large body wrapped around hers to keep her warm. Shane's long arm around her waist to hold her close. Shane's steady breathing to lull her to sleep in the first place.

She really hadn't a hope in hell of sleeping, had she?

Which meant she had thinking time.

Easing back until she was fully supported by the sofa, she focused her gaze on the curtains and let a list of queries form.

There was a lot of new information now. Like the fact that Shane's 'love 'em and leave 'em reputation' probably did stem from his past experiences. What age had he been when his father had left? Had he felt it as deeply as she'd felt the loss of her own father? Had he ever seen him again?

Finn had always assumed that *both* his parents were dead.

But if his lack of commitment was so deeply ingrained, why had he been so determined to persuade her he wasn't going anywhere?

She'd been on the money when it came to his leaving the fire brigade. Realistically she had used it only as a delaying tactic. But although she had known he wouldn't leave, she hadn't known the full reason why.

Or had she, deep down?

She had always known the bond that existed in the service, the common memories of experiences that no one outside their group could ever understand. But she hadn't known that to Shane they were almost a substitute family, one he knew he could rely upon to always be there and so trusted himself to be bonded to. He would never, ever give that up. For any woman, would he?

But if that was the case, then why had he been prepared to risk testing that bond by breaking some stupid rule that apparently they all considered written in stone?

The man was a set of contradictions. He said so little about the things that really mattered, but would make love to her with the skill and generosity of a lover who truly cared about pleasuring his mate before himself.

And as for the times when she had woken up and found him staring at her with that gentle smile on his face and softness in his eyes that practically said—

Finn sat bolt upright on the sofa, her eyes wide and her heart thumping so loudly in her chest that she could hear it in her ears.

He couldn't, could he?

Not Shane Dwyer, the love-'em-and-leave-'em guy! And it would be so much better if he didn't really, right? Because that wasn't what she wanted, was it?

Finn's breathing sped up.

No. It wasn't as if she would want him to be. Because, well, if he was, then that meant that when she left him she'd have really hurt him.

He hadn't looked hurt. He'd looked resigned.

Yes, that was it, calm and resigned. He hadn't looked as if she'd just stomped all over his heart with her size six feet.

Her breathing continued to come in quick, ragged breaths, and suddenly the room really wasn't all that cold. She flapped a hand in front of her face.

But if he really was hurting *would* he have shown her? After all, she'd made it plain from the start that she wasn't interested in getting that involved. And she'd meant it.

Yes, she had!

She'd meant it because she couldn't face the possibility of losing him. And she'd been right about that. Because she really couldn't. Even though she'd just, well, let him *be* lost to her.

But at least that had been her choice, *right*? She couldn't change her own past any more than she could change his. That was just the way things were.

The way she felt was deeply ingrained, was an imprint on her that had been present for most of her life. She really couldn't wait at home for him every day and eat herself up inside. *Waiting.*

She wasn't strong enough for that. Much as she'd like to be. But with her luck—

She'd just set her own house on fire, for crying out loud!

And if she wasn't strong enough to get over the fear of losing him, to take a chance on caring about someone *that* much...

Well, then realistically she didn't deserve him.

He deserved more than her just letting him go without a full explanation, though. He deserved an understanding of how she felt and why it was better for them to leave it be. Because if he *felt*—

Well, if he felt anything and she'd hurt him then he deserved to know that it wasn't just him that felt that way and it wasn't just him that was hurting.

They both needed a better form of closure than she'd left them with.

With the decision made, she moved swiftly, hauling on clothes over the top of her pyjamas and slipping trainers onto her feet.

She needed to see him.

CHAPTER FOURTEEN

SHANE had never actually been in his own house on his own before. Funny how he'd never thought about it.

It was only when the place was empty and he hadn't even the energy to switch on the TV for background noise that he noticed.

It was silent.

For someone who worked in an environment full of noise and people it was a shock to the system. And, worse still, it meant his mind had peace and quiet to think in.

But when all thinking did was lead him round and round in circles and back to the same damn subject every time, he had enough of silence.

So he marched to the stereo and put on some good, old-fashioned, angry rock music.

Which meant, coming back out of the kitchen with a beer, he was caught off guard to find Finn standing at the doorway staring at him. Off guard because he hadn't expected to see her and off guard because, quite simply, he hadn't heard her come in.

She looked nervous as hell.

What was she doing back?

For a brief second he was so pleased to see her he didn't

care what had brought her back. But he'd been walking round with an ache in his chest all afternoon and the fact that seeing her reminded him of it made him angry.

So he scowled at her. 'You leave some stuff behind?'

Finn had to raise her voice to the same yell level as his, 'No. I came to talk to you.'

'We don't have anything to talk about.'

'Yes!' With a sigh she stepped over to the stereo and turned the volume down, adjusting her voice level to something more civilized. '*We do*. We can't just leave this the way it is.'

'As in over, you mean?'

'As in, the *way* that it ended. I need you to talk to me, really talk to me.'

Shane could see the plea in her eyes from way across the room. 'To make you feel better about it?' He waved a nonchalant hand in the air. 'Forget about it.'

'I can't.'

'Oh, no, you don't.' He suddenly got what she was doing. 'You're here to do some female "understanding what happened thing", right? You were the one who always said it wouldn't last, remember?'

'I remember. And I remember you being the one to push for me to try. Why did you do that?'

'Nope.' He shook his head. 'You're not sucking me into a post-mortem, Finn. Leave it be.'

Still watching her with a cold gaze, he saw how her throat convulsed as she swallowed, saw how she blinked hard while she thought what to say next.

So he saved her the bother. 'What do you want me to say to you? That I'm sorry it ended like this? I'm sorry. It's messy right now and we both know it.'

'But why—?'

'Leave it be. I mean it.' Looking at her was getting to be tough, so he let his eyes stray to the sofa. 'I've done plenty of post-mortems before this and they don't make a blind bit of difference.'

She waited until he was sitting down, his back to her as he put his long legs up on the coffee-table.

'You're angry at me.'

'What does it matter now whether I am or not?'

A frustrated sound escaped her throat and she walked round so she could see his face. 'It matters to me.'

'Why?'

'Because I can't live with knowing I hurt you by not trying more.'

His laughter was bitter. 'Oh, good. This is a sympathy visit, then.'

'Don't be ridiculous!'

'I'm not being ridiculous. You've come over here to make sure that poor wee Shane, the commitment-phobic bloke, isn't all torn up that the first relationship he fancied having a go at went pear-shaped. And took a big chunk of the rest of his life with it.'

He was tired of sitting, and tired of trying to pretend that everything he'd just said wasn't true. So he stood up, thumped his beer bottle down on the coffee-table and towered over her, leaning his face close to hers. 'Go home, Finn.'

Finn merely raised her chin and looked at him with glittering eyes.

And Shane's heart cracked open in his chest.

'Maybe you didn't come over here to talk at all.' He seized hold of her arm and tilted his face closer, his mouth hovering over hers. 'Maybe you came for a different goodbye.'

'You son-of-a—'

His mouth silenced her with a hard, angry kiss. Finn struggled, tried to pull back from his searing lips, but he merely raised his other hand to the back of her head and held her in place. She tried using her free hand to push him away, but he pulled her closer.

It was only when she met anger with anger, kissed him back with equal force, that he tore his mouth from hers, his blue eyes glinting dangerously as he spoke in a hoarse whisper.

''Cos this is what we do best, isn't it? This is the only time that you forget what I am and let yourself go.'

'There's more to it than this.'

'But not enough for you to stay.'

Her breasts heaving against his chest, her eyes fixed on his, she let the confession of a lifetime out. Because there was only one truth left really. Now that she'd seen him again, kissed him again. 'I love you, Shane. That's why I can't stay.'

His breath caught. Staring for a long, silent while, he eventually answered her. 'If you loved me you wouldn't want to leave.'

'If I stayed I'd end up hating you.' She fought her way through tears. She was *so* not going to let herself cry. 'I'd try to be strong; I would. But every time you went out that door I'd be scared stupid. And even if you came home every time I'd have eaten a little piece of myself away worrying. Until I was so eaten up that I didn't feel anything any more. And I'd hate you for that one day.'

Untwisting her arm from behind her back, he asked her in a low voice, 'Was it that bad? When your dad died?'

'Yes.' A harsh sob caught in her throat as she looked away from the softness in his eyes.

She found herself studying the epaulette on his shirt, then her eyes dropped down to the 'Dublin City Fire Brigade' emblazoned in red letters on one side of his chest. 'He was my hero when I was a kid. A big giant of a man who came home every day in a shirt the same as the one you're wearing right now. And everything about him just seemed so big and brave to me.'

The hand on the back of her head eased, began a soothing caress on her scalp, and he felt her lean back into it.

'It was my mum who was the strict one, the one who laid down the law and forced us to do the things we didn't want to do. But when my dad came home the house changed. It got filled up with laughter and fun.' She smiled through the tears that streaked down her face.

'He used to lift me up and swing me. Every time he came home. He would lift me up and swing me round and round 'til I was dizzy and squealing. So I used to wait by the front door when I knew he was coming home, so I was the first one that saw him.'

Shane watched as her hand rose and her forefinger traced the lettering on his shirt.

'I was at the door when the men came in their dress uniforms. I can remember looking past them for my daddy. But he wasn't there. And when my mum came to the front door she started to cry before they even spoke.'

When her voice broke on the last words Shane couldn't bear it. He hauled her into his arms and held her close, feeling her pain as if it were his own. Hurting simply because she hurt.

'I didn't know what was happening. I remember Conor trying to take me out of the room. But I wouldn't go. And the men said all these things like how great a firefighter he was and how he'd been very brave and what a loss it was for everyone. And I still didn't understand. Then there were people all over the house, making cups of tea and talking in low voices. And I still didn't get it.' She let large tears soak his chest, her chin resting against the lettering.

'And I waited by the door. I waited by the door for him to come home and swing me. And he never came.'

Shane felt his breathing growing ragged beneath her cheek. He was glad she was telling him all of it. That she cared enough about him to want him to hear it. But while she shook against his body and the emotion was so raw in her voice it brought back memories of his own.

Made him think about the feelings he'd never shared with anyone else. Not so openly and honestly.

'I watched my mum disappear for a long while. I guess I was too young for her to talk to, but I wasn't so young that I didn't notice how she would cry when she didn't think we could hear her. Then she stopped crying and she went quiet and that was worse. It took a long time for the house to stop being quiet.'

Her breathing steadied and Shane felt her fighting for control.

'As I got older I understood better what she'd lost. And hurting the way I did I could only imagine how bad it was for her. I just *can't,* I just can't do that. Not when I already know what it will feel like. I'm not strong enough. And you deserve better than that.'

Then she stopped talking.

Shane held her for a long while, blinking as he stared into the middle distance. It would be easy to let the words out and tell her how he felt about her in that moment. But while he held her he knew that loving her as he did meant wanting what was best for her. He couldn't give her a written guarantee that nothing bad would ever happen to him, could he?

And knowing now how much she had been hurt he couldn't put her through the same thing again. It would be selfish, wouldn't it?

He cleared his throat. 'You're strong Finn McNeill. If you weren't you wouldn't have come over here to tell me all this so that I understood.'

'I couldn't let go without you knowing.'

Long arms squeezed around her. 'Knowing doesn't make it any easier to let you go.' He leaned his head down against hers, buried his face in her hair to mumble, 'I can't change who I am.'

'I wouldn't let you try.' It wouldn't be who he was. And if he wasn't who he was she might not love him so much.

Pressing a kiss against her hair, he rested his cheek against her head for a moment before she tilted it back to look up at him.

Summoning every ounce of self-control he had, he smiled at her. 'So, here we are, then.'

She smiled a sad smile in response to the low words.

Loosening his arms, he leaned back to make enough room to bring his hands up. He framed her face, his thumbs touching the edges of her swollen lips. Then he leaned closer, looking into her eyes.

'I'm not good with words, Finn, you know that. Not the important kind anyway. So I'll just do this my way.'

Finn held her breath while his head descended, his eyes not closing as his mouth settled on hers. Unlike the previous angry kiss that had been searing and possessive, this one started out like a whisper.

And it tore at her aching heart.

She moaned softly, brought her hands to his face in a mirror of his, with her thumbs touching the corners of his mouth. And she kissed him back equally softly, tracing the shape of his mouth from thumb to thumb and back again.

His thumbs moved, joining his fingertips in a slow, sensual tracing of the contours of her face. Up to her temples, over the curves of her eyebrows, sweeping over her eyelids to close them. Down over her cheekbones, lingering again on the edges of her mouth and then over the line of her jaw where it tilted up towards his face.

She let her hands move from his face to his chest, where she flattened her palms so she could feel his heart beating. She sighed against his lips, her head tilting back as he moved from her mouth to her jaw, from her jaw to the length of her neck, lingering on the pulse that beat at its base.

'*Shane.*'

'Yes.' The word was a whisper against her skin.

'Make love to me.'

His head lifted and he took her hand without saying a word, led her towards the stairs.

In his room he took his time, kissing every inch of skin he uncovered as he undressed her while he allowed her to take her time undressing him. Then, clothes in two piles on the wooden floor, he eased her back on the bed so slowly it was almost as if she were floating.

Of all the times they'd made love before, to Finn it was the most agonizing. Every touch, every kiss, every caress was a goodbye.

And happening so slowly it was excruciatingly painful to her heart.

He hadn't said the words to her. But skilful as she'd already known he was before, he'd never made love to her with such sweetness. He spent what felt like hours on her breasts, tracing their shape with gentle fingers, suckling on her turgid nipples until they ached.

When she tried to give the same attention to him, he merely pushed her back into the soft mattress and continued to caress her.

When she tried to reach between their bodies for the hard length of him, he tilted his hips and pressed himself closer to her side.

And all the while he kissed and licked and suckled so that by the time he pressed a long finger between her thighs she was wet and ready.

In the brief second it took for him to reach for protection she fixed her eyes on his. As she had when they'd made love for the first time. And she kept them fixed when he came back to her, when his fingers coaxed her legs wide and he settled into her body with deliberate slowness.

Finn knew in the moment that his pelvis hit hers, when he was buried as deep as he could go, that she would never make love with anyone else and feel such a soul-deep connection.

She loved him that much.

By the time he was moving with her, her hips rising to meet each thrust, tears were seeping from the corners of her eyes and onto the pillow. And when her body had clamped around his and she could hear her blood roaring in her ears she was weeping.

His body went tight, the muscles in his back bunching beneath her hands and he groaned, long and loud. Then he dropped onto her, his body spent.

And with his head buried in the curve of her neck he held onto her, whispering words she couldn't hear. But she didn't need to hear them to know what he was saying.

CHAPTER FIFTEEN

SHANE'S first meeting with Eddie was every bit as rough as he'd expected it would be. It took a few days with their shift pattern, and he had been hoping it would happen before the first shift they had together. Because it wouldn't make for much of a working relationship otherwise, and he really didn't want the pair of them hauled in front of the O.I.C. to explain the problem.

So when he finished a fifteen-hour night shift he wasn't completely surprised to see Eddie in the locker room.

But, prepared as he'd thought he would be, he hesitated nevertheless.

He had wanted his wits about him when they talked. And truth be told, he was wrecked. He hadn't slept much the last few nights and it had been a long shift.

Eddie's head rose and their eyes clashed across the room.

When he didn't get up off the bench Shane braved a few steps closer. 'We need to talk, mate.'

'I have nothing to say to you.'

'Well, you can listen, then.'

He laughed harshly. 'The hell I will.'

Shane watched as he stood up, shoved his trainers into

his locker and slammed the door shut with more force than necessary.

'You'll listen, Eddie. 'Cos at the end of the day we have to work together and we need to talk about this to be able to do that.'

'I can make sure I'm never on a shift with you again.'

'Don't be daft. It'll happen some time.'

Eddie glared at him, seeming to wrestle with what he was saying, and then leaned his face closer to Shane's to spit out, 'You should never have touched her!'

'Eddie—'

'There are dozens of women out there you could have had, and have done!'

Shane sighed. 'Nice and all as it would be for me to be the stud you *think* I am, it's not actually all that many. And it hasn't been *any* for a long while.'

'So in a drought you decided to sleep with my sister?'

He scowled at Eddie's reasoning. 'Don't be so ridiculous! You think if all it was was a quick roll that I'd have picked *Finn* to have it with?'

Two firefighters for the morning shift froze in the doorway at the sound of raised voices. 'What's going on?'

Eddie pointed at them. 'Get out.'

Shane glanced over at them and said in a calmer voice, 'Give us a minute, would you, lads?'

When they were gone he turned back to Eddie, just as Eddie swung for him. Shane dodged, grabbed his arm and shoved him back against the lockers. 'Damn it, Eddie, knock it off! I'm not gonna have a fight with you.'

Eddie swore viciously and fought to get off the lockers.

With them pretty much of equal height and build it took a few minutes of ungraceful struggling before Shane had

him stilled, his forearm over Eddie's shoulders to hold
him still.

'Bloody hell, Eddie, stop a minute and listen. This
wasn't just some quick shag! I *love* her.'

Eyes wide, Eddie froze. 'You *what*?'

Shane's hold loosened, his voice flat. 'You heard me.'

It took a long, tense moment of determined staring
before Eddie realized he was telling the truth. And Shane
knew him well enough to know when he knew.

So he let go and stepped back, sitting down on the bench
facing him.

Eddie straightened his uniform, his eyes still on Shane's
face, 'You love her?'

Shane nodded slowly, his tongue pushing against the
inside of his bottom lip.

'This is serious, then?' Eddie shook his head, running
both hands over his hair while he looked around the small
room. 'What am I saying? This is you. It's serious if *you're*
saying *that*.'

'It *was* serious. It's over. I just couldn't have you not
knowing it meant something.'

All too familiar green eyes settled back on his face, 'It's
over? For sure?'

Another slow nod.

Quirking his brows in surprise, Eddie turned round and
sat down beside him. In a synchronicity borne of familiarity they both leaned forward and rested their forearms
on their thighs.

Eddie took a breath. 'What happened?'

Shane shrugged. 'She didn't want to be involved with
a firefighter. It was too much for her after your dad.'

'Yeah, I know about that. I have to call her every time

I finish a shift so she knows I'm in one piece. That's a lot of calls over the years.'

Shane glanced at him in surprise. He'd just thought it was something they did because they were close. 'You never told me that.'

'Yeah, well, we don't talk about it that much. She broke down not long after I told her I was going in for the training. We talked all night and the only thing I could do was promise her the calls if she promised to remember what a charmed life I lead. I've never so much as broken a bone and that was a miracle itself in our house. Conor and Niall could be right so-and-so's. And as for Finn. Well, you've seen the running disaster her life can be.'

'Phone calls won't do it this time.'

'I don't think they would. It's a real big deal for her, you know, especially with her luck.'

'I know.' He looked down at the floor. 'Now.'

Eddie studied the top of his head. 'It would have to be equally as big a deal for her to get involved with you.'

'Yeah.'

'And you just let her go?'

He didn't answer.

'Well, then you're a fool.'

Shane's face turned in his direction. 'You don't want me involved with her. It wasn't my style, remember? Like father like son…'

Eddie grimaced. 'Okay, that one was uncalled for. I'm sorry about that. If you'd just sat down and talked to me I might not have been such a nutter about it when I found out. It was the fact the two of you did it all Secret Service style that I had the biggest problem with.' He sighed, thought for a moment.

'But that was before I knew all this stuff. If Finn got that involved with you knowing what you do for a living, then it's as serious for her as it is for you. And that's a whole other story.'

'Was.'

He glanced at Shane from the corner of his eye. 'I have to say I'm disappointed in you, Shane.'

Shane sighed. 'Great. I think I liked it better when you hated my guts.'

'No, c'mon, now. You've gone all this time without a serious relationship and now that you go and fall for my sister, you just let her wander off?' He made little walking legs in the air with his fingers. 'I thought you had more fight than that.'

Shane stared in disgust as the walking fingers came back to dangle off Eddie's knees. Then he sighed and rubbed his hands over his face. 'I need more sleep before I have the rest of this talk.'

'Tough.'

'Look, Eddie, I've had a really rubbish couple of days and the only way I've got through them is by telling myself I'll find a way round this. I just haven't found it yet.'

'Well, then, tell your uncle Eddie what you've come up with so far and with my insider info we'll work it out between us.'

Shane smiled a lopsided smile. 'Not this time.'

'Aw, c'mon. How many choices have you come up with on your own?'

'How about a choice between Finn and the fire brigade?'

Eddie swore again.

'Exactly. I understand why she feels the way she does, the history behind it. And I can't give her up, Eddie. But I just don't know that I can give this up either. It's not like I'm built for a desk job.'

'You'd look like you were sittin' at one of those wee desks you get in primary school.'

Shane laughed.

'So, what you gonna do?'

He dropped his head again. 'Dunno yet. But I'll figure something out.'

They sat in silence for a while. Then Shane turned his head and asked, 'So, are we good again, you and me?'

Eddie pursed his mouth. 'I still owe you a good swing for going behind my back. That stung, pal.'

Shane mimicked the pursing. Waiting.

'But we've been friends a long while. Longer than you've been in love with my sister, and I guess that counts for something.' He took a long breath. 'Tell you what: just sort it out with her, do it right, and we'll forget about the way it happened. Okay?'

'Okay with me.'

It was the second worst Christmas she'd ever had. She'd made it through the couple of days running up to it by working every hour that had needed work done and had consequently been so exhausted she had almost fallen onto Kathy's sofa bed at night.

But that hadn't stopped her bad dream from coming back with monotonous regularity. It occurred to her that she hadn't had it the entire time she'd been sharing a bed with Shane. Which was a tad ironic.

She truly resented everything about that dream now. All right, so a shrink could probably have made money out of interpreting it for her, but it didn't really take a genius.

All it was was her obsession with firefighters getting hurt. Her subconscious mind's way of keeping her on track.

While her conscious mind spent every waking moment obsessing about the one firefighter she missed so much it was like having had a limb removed. Without an anaesthetic.

The only saving grace had been that she'd managed to avoid her brother while she'd been so busy with everything else.

Unfortunately that meant she ended up with him staring at her all the way through Christmas dinner. Which annoyed her so much that by the time the heavy fruit pudding was being handed around she lifted her eyebrows and challenged him outright to say something.

'Quiet round here without Shane, isn't it, Mam?'

Finn wanted to kill him.

'It's a shame he couldn't make it. I'll have to send him up a plate.'

'Finn could drop it in when she gets back to Dublin, couldn't you, Finn?'

Finn glared.

'Take his presents as well, pet.' Her mother patted her shoulder on the way past. 'I got him a lovely Aran sweater this year and big long thermal socks.'

She took a deep breath and prayed for Easter to come.

There was no point in trying to leave the table to hide in her old room, because her mother would come and find her. And there was no point in arguing with Eddie because her mother would want to know what it was about.

So she just sat still and said nothing.

Somehow she got through the rest of the day. She even told herself she'd done a pretty good job of smiling when she was supposed to smile and talking when she was spoken to.

Though for the first time in her life she was deeply relieved when her brothers and their partners started to leave.

She stood in the hallway, swept along in the madness of them all going. Then Eddie stood in front of her with the same studious look on his face.

With a bright smile pinned to her face she said a cheery, 'Bye, Eddie.'

Because she really *was* glad he was going.

He blinked a couple of times and then kissed her on the cheek. 'Tell Shane I said hello.'

Finn sighed as he left.

Her mother closed the door after she'd finished waving and smiled, 'Right, then. You can help me clean up and you can tell me what's wrong.'

'There's nothing wrong.'

'Aye, and I'm the Queen of England.' She linked her arm with her daughter's and steered them into the kitchen. 'You've been quiet as the grave all day long and your brother has been staring at you like you have two heads.'

Sitting at the breakfast bar Finn poured two glasses of wine and gave in to the inevitable with a deep breath. 'Can I ask you a question first?'

'Of course you can.' She smiled encouragingly as she lifted a glass and perched on a matching stool.

'It's about Dad.'

Her face transformed into the wistful smile that she always wore when she talked about her husband. 'Ask away.'

'How did you cope?'

'I coped like everyone copes. I let myself grieve. Then I kept going until it didn't hurt so much any more. It doesn't go away, you know. You just learn to live with it, is all.'

Finn watched as her mother's hands automatically

reached for a roll of cling film while she talked. Without breaking her speech, she began wrapping plates of leftovers for the fridge.

So Finn continued, 'I didn't mean after it happened. I meant when he was going to work every day. Weren't you scared for him?'

'Oh, Lord, every day.' She laughed softly. 'I used to drive your dad mad asking about every call they were on.'

Finn blinked at her in silent amazement. 'But how did you not end up torturing yourself over it?'

Her mother's shoulders shrugged. 'I had all of you. You kept me busy most of the time, and the rest of the time I was just happy that he kept coming home. If I'd have let myself think he wasn't coming back every time I couldn't have got through the day.'

'But then he didn't.'

'No.' Her hands stilled. 'No, he didn't and no amount of worrying can prepare you for how that feels. But I had my time with him, sweetheart, and I wouldn't have missed out on that.'

If Finn hadn't been there to witness the aftermath she wouldn't have known just how devastating it was from her mother's synopsis of it. She shook her head slightly in wonder.

'But what about if you'd known what it would feel like beforehand? Would you still have put yourself through it?'

Moira McNeill's astute hazel eyes focused firmly on her daughter's face. 'Now what on earth has you asking something like that?'

She shrugged and looked down at her wineglass. 'We've never talked about it.'

'We've talked about your dad lots before. But you've

never asked me that. You know I loved your dad more than life. I still love him.'

'I know.' She aimed a small smile at her, her eyes shimmering. 'Me too. I just need to know, Mum. It's important. If you could go back and do it all again, knowing what you do now, how could you have coped with it?'

'Well, for goodness' sake. If we all worried about the bad things that might happen and forgot about the good we might find we'd never leave the house, would we?'

The reasoning made her feel vaguely infantile. 'It's not as simple as that. If you know the chances of experiencing that much pain exist then it's only natural you would do something to protect yourself against it.'

There was a brief pause. 'Has this got something to do with Shane Dwyer?'

Finn's eyes widened, then narrowed. 'Did Eddie say something to you?'

'No, but if it's something to do with Shane, then it explains why he's not here and why you and Eddie were glaring all the way through dinner.'

Caught. 'All right, it's something to do with Shane.'

Her mother's face transformed. 'Oh, I am pleased! He's such a dish. I had hoped when he was looking at you the way he did last Christmas…'

'Mum!'

'If I was twenty years younger…' She fanned her face with her hand.

'*Mum!*'

'And it must be serious for him to go getting involved with you, what with his family history and all.'

'Oh, for crying out loud! Am I the *only* one that didn't know that about him?'

'He's not much of a talker, that boy.'

'He talked to *you*.' She tilted her head and raised her eyebrows sarcastically.

'Well, yes, but that's different. I'm like an adoptive mother to him. I think it was his third or fourth Christmas here when we got to talking about his mother. And I managed to coax the rest out of him.'

Which was more than Finn had managed. Why was it so very difficult for him to communicate with her on any level other than—?

'I think he carries a lot of that around with him still. It's not easy when your father has another family and ignores his first child completely. Made him wary of getting close to people, I think. But everyone has something they carry about these days, don't they?' She paused.

'Are you telling me you're worried about getting involved with him because of what happened with your dad?'

Finn paused, swallowed down a bubble of emotion and then managed a nod.

'Auch, sweetheart!' Her mother was around the breakfast bar in a flash and had an arm around her shoulders before the first tear had escaped her eyes. 'You can't let what happened to your dad ruin your chance at being happy. Your dad would hate that!'

'I just don't know how to stop it. If anything happened to Shane—'

'Nothing might ever happen to him. And you're a firefighter's girl!' She squeezed her shoulders tight. 'You're made of sterner stuff than that.'

'No, I'm not. There's still a part of me standing by that front door and hoping Dad will come back through it.'

'Oh, goodness, I'd forgotten how you used to do that. He

used to swing you so high that sometimes I thought he'd hit your head off the ceiling.' She smiled down at her daughter.

'You were his little girl. He loved his boys, but you were different. I think all men are that way with their wee girls. You wait and see, your Shane will be the same. And unless I'm mistaken, all the more determined to be a good father after what he went through himself.'

The thought of Shane swinging a little dark-haired girl in the air made her catch her breath. It was an achingly beautiful image. Especially for someone who hadn't even considered having children until her biological clock was ticking *really* loudly.

Her shoulders were squeezed again.

Then her mother reached across for a piece of kitchen roll and handed it to her before she sat down on a stool beside her. 'Wait'll I tell you something my darlin'. Your dad would kick you from here to next week if he saw you making yourself sad when you didn't have to. He lived every day the way he wanted to. He loved me, he loved his kids, he loved the men he worked with and what he did. And that made him a very happy man while he was here. You can't ask much more than that.'

Finn blew her nose loudly into the kitchen roll.

'When you love someone it's a risk. It always is. But that's just life. You're the one that has to make the choice to live it.'

She crumpled. She wanted to make that choice, she really, really did. Just how much of a self-destructive idiot was she?

'We should have had a talk like this a long time ago.'

'Yes, we should.'

The arm snaked around her shoulders again. 'That boy needs someone like you in his life as much as you need him. Maybe more. Because he never knew love growing up like you did. If you love him, then you have to take a chance. That's all there is to it.'

Finn sat on the stool in her mother's embrace as the tears dried and she blew her nose again. Why was it that, even as a fully grown independent woman, it still took wise words and a hug from her mother for her to find the courage to believe in herself enough to admit the truth?

It wasn't just losing Shane that scared her. It was her own ability to love someone that much and allow herself to trust the emotion.

She'd probably been in love with him for years. It wasn't him she'd been fighting. It had been herself. Maybe part of loving was letting go of fear and trusting in whatever came next.

CHAPTER SIXTEEN

AFTER three days at her mum's Finn felt as if she'd done months of therapy. She'd always known she had things from her dad's death that she hadn't ever dealt with, or talked through with her mum.

And, ironically, she had the love for another firefighter to thank for that breakthrough.

Now all she had to do was figure out what to do about that firefighter.

Because if she was going to try and work on doing away with half a lifetime of being scared, then she was going to need some help. And having convinced him so thoroughly that she wasn't strong enough to stay with him, she was going to have quite a job convincing him that she wasn't strong enough to be without him.

But what she was going to say completely escaped her already exhausted mind. She had to get it right this time. She couldn't keep running to him and then running away. And realistically *he* wasn't one that was good with words either so *one* of them had to get it right when it mattered most.

Maybe she should just make an effort to show him in

the way he was good at showing her? Every day. Every day and at least a couple of times a night.

Until he believed her need for him was greater than her fear of losing him.

It was a stinker of a day to make the trip back to Dublin. Of the varying different types of rain available to the connoisseur in Ireland she was driving through the sideways variety. The sideways, hit-the-ground-and-bounce-up-to-get-you-a-second-time variety.

The traffic picked up as she paid through the toll-bridge, dozens of cars vying to get ahead as they streamed back into the lanes of the motorway. And it was getting dark, the heavy rain clouds and sideways rain obscuring any light from the evening sky.

Finn had just allowed her thoughts to stray from Shane long enough to wish she'd left a couple of hours earlier when a car veered in front of her from the fast lane.

She swore, stood on the brakes and felt her car slide on the wet surface.

Her heart caught as the nutcase in front then pulled back out into the fast lane. Right in front of another car.

And after that everything moved into slow motion. Until her cars were filled with the sickening sound of metal hitting metal.

Slow motion could only have been a few minutes. And then there was silence.

She knew there was silence so that meant, technically, she was aware it was silent. Which meant she was okay. And after a tentative check on her wriggling toes and fingers she knew she was still in one piece.

So she looked around her.

She could see headlights pointed the wrong way, one car

on its side. And her immediate instinct was to get out and help. To try and do what she could for anyone else who might be hurt. It was an instinctive, automatic reaction.

Which might have struck her as ironic for someone who had spent half their life trying to persuade others to give up doing the same thing, if around about that moment she hadn't realized she was stuck.

'Oh, gimme a *break* here!'

Shane was on the second appliance called to the scene. Eddie had been on the first crew and was the first person he met when they parked up and got out.

'Where do they need us?'

'The paramedics have everyone that needs to be stabilized looked at.' Eddie's face was grim below his yellow helmet. 'We're cutting one out down the bottom now. No fatalities.'

Shane nodded and started forwards only to be stopped by a gloved hand. He looked back at Eddie. 'What?'

'Don't panic, okay?'

He felt a bubble of panic. '*Why*?'

'Finn—' It was as far as he got before he had to grip harder. 'She's okay. I've already been over there and she's been checked out.'

Shane yanked his arm again.

'Wait a minute!' Eddie's voice rose above approaching sirens. 'Seriously, *she's fine*! She's a bit bumped up but she's fine. When I got over there the paramedic was trying to chat her up.'

A thunderous look was aimed his way.

Releasing the braced arm, he held his hands up in surrender. 'Not my fault.'

'Where is she?'

'Over by the bridge. Her car is stuck against the pillar. She won't be cut out for a bit 'cos the others take priority.'

But the words were already fading into the distance as Shane took off at the run.

His heart thundered as his eyes found the familiar sight of her car. There were lights set up and in the rain he could see the upward bend in the car's roof, but it was still in one piece and didn't look to be in as bad shape as the one the other crew were working on.

For the first time in his career, Shane ignored those in worse shape, knowing they were being taken care of by others.

He was only concerned with one person.

As he got closer a tall paramedic was stepping back from the passenger door. Shane's fists bunched as he approached him.

The paramedic stepped towards him, took one look at his face and smiled. 'I guess you're Shane.'

Shane nodded, his eyes on the front of the car.

The man's voice lowered. 'The other firefighter said you might appear. He also said it would be good if I wasn't chatting up your girl when you got here.'

'He was right.' Shane's eyes strayed to him. He gave him the once-over and just as quickly dismissed him. 'How's she doing?'

'She's great—bit bruised, I'd say. Leg is stuck but it's not broken or cut. Her vitals are all fine and she has a sense of humour about her predicament, so I'd say that was a good sign. Just waiting for your guys to get her out now and I'll check her over again to be sure before she goes to the hospital.' He grinned. 'She's a real trooper.'

Shane smiled a small, warmer smile. 'I know. You're sure she's okay?'

'Yep.'

He took a deep breath to steady himself.

Okay. Calm, Shane. She's fine. She's fine and she's stuck there.

Right then. In that case she was getting a talking to. Enough was enough.

Finn had accepted the fact that she wasn't going anywhere. Had finished watching raindrops drifting down her cracked windscreen and was contemplating what other disasters could possibly come her way when there was movement at her passenger door.

Large boots were followed by long legs and finally a huge fluorescent striped jacket appeared beside her.

It couldn't be Eddie, as he'd already been over for a wee visit, so that could only mean…

She looked upwards as the helmet turned her way.

Shane smiled. 'Well, hello.'

With a small, resigned burst of laughter, she shook her head and leaned it back against the head rest. 'Hello.'

'Glad you drive a Volvo now, aren't you?'

'Yes, I most definitely am.'

'You're on a roll at the minute.'

'I did tell Kathy these things come in threes, but she wouldn't listen.'

He turned his head and looked out of her cracked windscreen. 'That's them done now then. You'll be safe to leave the house for another while.'

Finn chanced a glimpse at his profile, so ridiculously

glad to see him that everything else seemed to fade into the background against it.

'Hope so. But then seein' as I don't have a house or a car now I might be forced to live on the street for a while.'

'Mmm.'

She watched him purse his mouth in thought, frustrated that he seemed so calm. Well, wasn't he just Mr Professional? She was about to open her mouth and say as much when—

'You scared me, Finn.' He turned his head and looked her straight in the eye, his voice stern. 'Locked indoors where I can keep an eye on you would be the best place for you.'

'I didn't do this on purpose. I was driving along minding my own business when some moron decided to play dodgems on the motorway!' She had lifted her head to give out to him, but flumped it back in frustration, wriggling the toes on her trapped leg as the paramedic had told her to.

'And now I'm stuck. Just stuck, that's all. In the words of someone I know: "It's no big deal".'

'Do you hurt anywhere?'

The question stopped her sarcasm dead. And she blinked a small look of reassurance in his direction, 'The nice paramedic already checked me out.'

'Oh, I *heard*.'

The look on his face made her smile. He was jealous. Jealous was good. Jealous was fantastically good. Almost worth getting her car crumpled for.

Though it was an extreme method of getting his attention.

Shane considered her face for a moment, then seemed to make a decision. He turned around on the seat, settling himself so his large body was facing hers in the intimate space.

'Right, well, if you're fine and you're stuck here for a while, then we're having a bit of a talk.'

Finn's eyes widened. 'You're going to take advantage of my predicament to talk to me? *You*, the amazing talking man who—'

'Finn, *shut up.*'

He said it so firmly, she shut up. Her mouth was a silent 'oh' of surprise.

'I've been working on what I was going to say to you when you got back to Dublin for days now and since you're stuck here you're gonna get it all in one go. So you need to shut up and listen.'

She snapped her mouth shut.

He pulled a glove off one hand and fished in a pocket under his jacket. Then he produced a folded piece of paper and waved it in front of her.

'I did some research to begin with, but it's useless now you're in here.' So he scrumpled it up and threw it out of the open door behind him. Then, pulling his glove back on, he tilted his helmet back on his head. 'So thanks for that. I'll just have to start with this…'

Head still resting on the head rest, but her face turned towards his, her eyes widened as he leaned in and placed a gentle, lingering kiss on her mouth.

Then, his face back a little from hers, he continued. Warm breath fanning her cheeks, he simply said, 'I love you, Finn McNeill.'

In a husky voice that said he meant it.

The world went still. Well, it did for Finn. He'd said it. He loved her. It was the most amazingly wonderful thing. So this was what it felt like to love and be loved in return. God, it felt *good*.

She blinked hard.

He waggled a gloved finger at her as he leaned back, 'You needn't think for one minute that I'm all that easy to get rid of. That paper—' the glove transformed from a waggling finger into a thumb that jerked back over his shoulder '—had firefighter fatality stats for the last fifty years on it. And they were a pain in the ass to get just so you know. I figured I needed the stats to show you the like-lihood of anything happening to me was slim. But seeing as you're here in an R.T.A. it doesn't matter a damn what they say. 'Cos statistically you're more likely to get killed on the roads in this country than I am doing what I do. 'Cos I prepare for my job, every day, and there's no way anyone can prepare for this.'

He paused. 'Now, if I thought for one second you were going to get into this kind of trouble every time you drove a car then there would be no way I'd let you out of the house for the next sixty years. But you know what?'

He didn't wait for an answer. 'A plane could fall on either of our heads tomorrow or a bus could run over us or any of a dozen things. The thing is, the way I see it, you don't spend your whole life waiting for something bad to happen when something as good as us comes along.'

Her blinking got harder.

The gloved finger waggled at her again as he frowned. 'Nah, and don't you dare go lookin' at me like you're gonna cry, 'cos I'm not done.'

'Shane, 'bout ten minutes, okay?'

He yelled back over his shoulder, 'Grand. We're fine in here.'

Finn blinked through moist eyes as he looked back at her. 'Now, where was I? Oh, yeah.' He leaned in again. 'I know that you're scared babe, I do. And I know why. What happened to your dad was the thing that every firefighter hopes will never happen to them. But doing this job isn't just doing a job, it's what I am and if I stopped doing it I'd be selling the both of us short. And, yes, it's probably a bigger deal for me than most, 'cos 'til I had the service I didn't know what it was like to be part of a family like that. A bunch of people who care about you even when you don't ask them to and who take your caring about them in return as a given. *For life.* I've never once felt in the service that I was less important because new family members came along.'

He thought for a split second. 'There *is* some stuff about my family for you to know, and I'll tell you about that as we go along, but I'm on the clock here. It's just a load of stuff about my dad skipping off to a new family and forgetting he had me.'

Finn watched in silence as he shrugged it off, literally. She wouldn't tell him she already knew, she wanted him to tell her in his own words, to share it so that she could hold him as he'd held her when she'd shared painful private memories.

'*So.* Anyway. Here's how I see it. I can't quit the job 'cos it would kill a part of me, and you're getting it all whether you want it or not. Hell, you've already got it. What I can do is make a promise to you to never do anything dumb, which I don't do anyway. I can't stop the very low percentage of accidents that do happen, but then, *obviously*—' the glove rose and waved in the air in front of his body '—neither can you.'

Finn found herself smiling.

He was actually making perfect sense in the same region of perfect sense that had been talked to her by her mother for the last few days. Bless him.

'I can promise you that we'll make every day count. That even when we row we'll have so much fun making up that we'll forget what we rowed about in the first place. That you'll never doubt for a minute that you're it for me, 'cos you are. When you get scared you're gonna say so and I'll hold onto you. And when I get scared—' his dimples flashed '—I'll pretty much do the same thing.'

When her eyebrows rose in disbelief he laughed. 'I have my moments. Five minutes ago being a good example.'

She laughed with him.

Then his voice dropped to a husky level that reminded her of tangled sheets and bodies wrapped around each other. 'No one has any guarantees these days. All I can do is tell you, you'll never have any regrets. I'll make bloody sure of that, trust me.'

There was the sound of voices getting closer to the car.

Shane aimed a glance out the back window. 'They're coming to get you out now, so I'll be quick.'

Finn chuckled.

His blue eyes were almost black again in the dim light but Finn didn't need to see to know there was infinite softness there; she could hear it in his voice. 'Thing is. You've got this impression that I'm some hero type 'cos of what I do. But it's you that's the hero. You got me to believe in something I never knew could happen for me. And now that you've rescued me from a string of useless relationships you're stuck with me. Full stop.'

She could feel her eyes filling again as he looked at her. Could honestly feel as if any second her heart would explode out of her chest.

That would be what happiness felt like, then.

It was like having someone lift her up and swing her round and round, endlessly.

'Say something.'

She waited a long moment. 'For someone who claims they're not much of a talker, you had a lot to say, didn't you?'

He shrugged. 'I've been thinking for a while.'

'Yeah.' She nodded. 'I got that impression.'

'We're gonna take the roof off, Shane.' Callum appeared at the passenger door with a fireproof sheet. Handing it in, he winked at Finn. 'Hey, Finn, how ya doin'? Long time no see.'

'Hi, Callum, you're looking well.'

'Ah, y'see now, nothing quite like a man in uniform.'

Shane shook his head. 'Mind your fingers on that big tin opener, won't you, Callum?'

Finn giggled as he spread the sheet over their heads. 'Aren't you going to get out?'

'Nah. Already told you. You're stuck with me.' He smiled before it went dim under the sheet. As the compressor started up, he raised his voice. 'So, you get all that?'

She moved her head closer and yelled back, 'I got that you love me and sixty years indoors and after that it went a wee bit blurry.'

'Well, so long as you got the important stuff.'

There was a loud creaking as they cut the roof off. Then another, followed by an equally loud sound of metal being bent.

All of which Shane distracted her from by kissing her with a kiss that spoke of heartfelt promises and lost time to be made up for.

When they came out of the sheet, rain was falling on their heads.

The compressor went silent as several firefighters gathered around to figure out where to safely free the steering column and Finn looked at Shane again.

He turned slowly, silhouetted by emergency lighting, rain falling off his helmet. And he took her breath away.

But not because of the way he looked in his work gear. Because he was Shane, and she loved him. She'd be an idiot not to want to make the most of her time with him. No matter how long that time was. And after everything he'd said, she felt stronger, had more faith in herself and her ability to love and be loved.

As if by loving her he had given her the faith she needed to get past her demons.

Or at least to give them a pretty good run for their money...

He smiled. 'So?'

'So?' She smiled back.

'What's your answer?'

'I wasn't aware you'd asked me a question.'

'I'm sure it was in there somewhere.'

She laughed. 'Maybe you should try asking me again.'

'Now, *babe*, you know I'm not good with words.' His eyes sparkled in the rain. 'Just say yes.'

Reaching out, she took a gloved hand in hers and squeezed. 'I love you.'

'Yeah.' His voice was seduction itself. 'I know.'

They sat and smiled at each other for a while.

Then Shane looked up at the faces around them. 'Right, then—' his voice rose '—any chance of you losers getting my fiancée outta this wreck so I can take her home?'

'Aw, Finn, what you marrying him for?'

'Ah, sure, some women will do anything to get themselves out of a car when they're stuck.'

Shane freed her hand, and pushed himself upright with a curse.

'Do I have to do everything round here? You lot need to read the manual when we get back to the station. I know there's one with pictures somewhere.'

Finn laughed as he stepped onto the bonnet as if he were taking a walk in the park, pushing Callum out of the way. She looked round at the faces that surrounded her while they tossed insults at each other. And finally noticed her brother's face amongst them.

Grinning at her.

Then, with a nod, he winked and handed up some equipment to Shane. 'Get a move on, then, *brother-in-law*.'

For Finn it was the first memory she could store in her heart from the beginning of the rest of her life. She'd taken up enough of her life obsessed with the worst.

And what better way to start all the good stuff than surrounded by the family she'd been born into? She had a feeling her dad would approve…

Though what he'd have had to say about the underwear incident would have been more than her ears would have stood.

Funny how fires had been the one thing she had hated all her life. And yet, in the end, had been the one thing that had given back to her what she'd been missing for half her life.

A great big lump of a firefighter as the centre of her world.

Finn had a feeling she'd definitely come to the end of her run of bad luck. She should have burnt those big pants much, much earlier.

REQUEST YOUR FREE BOOKS!

2 FREE NOVELS PLUS 2 FREE GIFTS!

PASSION GUARANTEED SEDUCTION

YES! Please send me 2 FREE Harlequin Presents® novels and my 2 FREE gifts. After receiving them, if I don't wish to receive any more books, I can return the shipping statement marked "cancel." If I don't cancel, I will receive 6 brand-new novels every month and be billed just $3.80 per book in the U.S., or $4.47 per book in Canada, plus 25¢ shipping and handling per book and applicable taxes, if any*. That's a savings of close to 15% off the cover price! I understand that accepting the 2 free books and gifts places me under no obligation to buy anything. I can always return a shipment and cancel at any time. Even if I never buy another book from Harlequin, the two free books and gifts are mine to keep forever.

106 HDN EEXK   306 HDN EEXV

Name   (PLEASE PRINT)

Address   Apt. #

City   State/Prov.   Zip/Postal Code

Signature (if under 18, a parent or guardian must sign)

Mail to the Harlequin Reader Service®:
IN U.S.A.: P.O. Box 1867, Buffalo, NY 14240-1867
IN CANADA: P.O. Box 609, Fort Erie, Ontario L2A 5X3

Not valid to current Harlequin Presents subscribers.

**Want to try two free books from another line?
Call 1-800-873-8635 or visit www.morefreebooks.com.**

* Terms and prices subject to change without notice. NY residents add applicable sales tax. Canadian residents will be charged applicable provincial taxes and GST. This offer is limited to one order per household. All orders subject to approval. Credit or debit balances in a customer's account(s) may be offset by any other outstanding balance owed by or to the customer. Please allow 4 to 6 weeks for delivery.

Your Privacy: Harlequin is committed to protecting your privacy. Our Privacy Policy is available online at www.eHarlequin.com or upon request from the Reader Service. From time to time we make our lists of customers available to reputable firms who may have a product or service of interest to you. If you would prefer we not share your name and address, please check here. ☐

HP07

HARLEQUIN *Presents*

BILLI❀NAIRES' BRIDES
by Sandra Marton

Pregnant by their princes...

Take three incredibly wealthy European princes
and match them with three beautiful, spirited women.
Add large helpings of intense emotion and passionate attraction.
Result: three unexpected pregnancies...and
three possible princesses—if those princes have their way....

THE ITALIAN PRINCE'S PREGNANT BRIDE
August 2007

THE GREEK PRINCE'S CHOSEN WIFE
September 2007

THE SPANISH PRINCE'S VIRGIN BRIDE

Prince Lucas Reyes believes Alyssa is trying to pretend
she's untouched by any man. Lucas's fiery royal blood is roused!
He'd swear she's pure uninhibited mistress material,
and never a virgin bride!

Available October wherever you buy books.

Look for more great Harlequin authors every month!